THE BABY-SITTERS CLUB

Jessi and the Dance School Phantom
Ann M. Martin

AN
APPLE
PAPERBACK

SCHOLASTIC INC.
New York Toronto London Auckland Sydney

The author gratefully acknowledges
Ellen Miles
for her help in
preparing this manuscript.

Cover art by Hodges Soileau

ISBN 0-590-44083-7

12 11 10 9 8 7 6 5 4 3 2   1 2 3 4 5 6/9

Printed in the U.S.A.   40

First Scholastic printing, March 1991

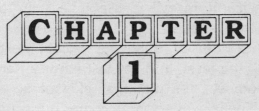

CHAPTER 1

"And now, mademoiselles, if you please: a *pas de bourrée couru, en cinquième,* with *port de bras,* ending in an *arabesque.* One at a time, please . . . and begin!" Mme Noelle banged her stick on the floor to emphasize her words.

A stranger might have thought they'd wandered into some other world — and in a way, they'd be right. A ballet studio *is* another world — a world where movement is everything, and where words are shorthand for what our bodies should be doing.

Pah deh boure-ay koo-roo? On sank-eeyem? With por deh brah? And an ara-besk? Sounds crazy, but what Mme Noelle, our teacher, wanted us to do was to move on our toes across the floor, holding our arms in graceful patterns, and end by standing on one toe with our arms held out to the sides. That's what all those words meant. They're French.

I don't speak French, but I know those

words, and a lot of others, because French is the language of ballet, and I've been studying ballet since I was four. I'm eleven now, so that's a long time!

"Jessica Romsey, please take your turn!" said Mme Noelle.

Jessica Romsey, that's me. Except most people call me Jessi, and my last name's Ramsey, not Romsey. It's just that elegant accent of Mme Noelle's; everything comes out sounding kind of — well, kind of fancy.

I closed my eyes for a second, picturing what I was about to do. I wanted to do the best *pas de bourrée* I'd ever done. Why? Because this was the final stage in the final auditions for a big production that was going to be put on by my ballet school. We were going to be putting on *The Sleeping Beauty*. And I was trying out for the lead!

I took a deep breath, let it out slowly, and rose onto my toes. Then I began. I was so focused that I was hardly aware of Mme Noelle's attention, but I knew she was watching every single muscle in my body, checking to make sure that I was in complete control.

Normally, as I *bourrée*'d past her, Madame would be making comments like, "Long neck, Mademoiselle Romsey!" or, "Use zee onkles!" (That's "ankles," just in case you were wondering.) But this wasn't a class. This was an audition. And I was on my own.

I finished the *bourrée* and went into an *arabesque*, stretching my arms gracefully (I hoped). Then I clomped off the stage area, my toe shoes clacking with every step.

I watched the other girls do what I'd done, one at a time. There are a lot of good dancers in my class, which makes sense — it is, after all, an advanced class. Take Mary Bramstedt, for example. Right then she was *bourrée*-ing across the floor, in perfect form. She always seems to be in perfect form. But I think (and this is just my personal opinion — I'd never say it out loud) that there's something missing when she dances. Something like — I know this might sound really silly but — passion. She's kind of like a robot, you know?

I don't think anyone could mistake me for a robot — and not just because I'm not always in perfect form. As far as I know, there aren't too many black robots running around — in fact, there are probably even fewer black robots than there are black ballerinas.

Luckily, there are a few black ballerinas now. Twenty years ago, there weren't any. And someone like me, with skin the color of cocoa and eyes like coal, could never have dreamed of joining a ballet company. But now I can dream. And it makes me glad, because I absolutely, positively *love* to dance.

So does Carrie Steinfeld, and it was showing as she did her *bourrée*. She's a great dancer — one of the best in the class. She's also one of the oldest students in the class, and she'll be graduating soon. This might be her last chance to get a starring role in a production — a role that would really give her an edge if she could add it to her résumé.

Without having had a role like Princess Aurora, the leading part in *The Sleeping Beauty*, Carrie might have a hard time getting into another dance school for older students. And she'd have hardly any chance at all of joining a ballet company. The ballet world is very competitive.

"Very nice, Mademoiselle Steinfeld," said Mme Noelle. I bit my lip. She hadn't said anything when I finished *my bourrée*. I tried not to worry about it. It might not mean a thing, after all.

I found Mme Noelle very intimidating when I first joined this school, back when my family moved to Stoneybrook, Connecticut. That was not too long ago, when my dad was transferred to the Stamford office of his firm. The move was tough on the whole family.

It was tough for the usual reasons — leaving friends and family, coming to a strange new place — but there were other reasons that made it even worse. The neighborhood we used to live in, in New Jersey, was completely integrated. So were the schools. But in Stoneybrook, it's different. Here there are very few black families. People just weren't used to seeing black faces — and they didn't make us feel too welcome. In fact, it was the opposite.

But over time, we've all made friends in Stoneybrook, and our lives have settled down. I'd have to say that my family is pretty happy here now. And for me, one of the best parts of the move was getting into this dance school. The school isn't actually *in* Stoneybrook — it's in Stamford, where my dad's office is. It's one of the best on the East Coast — if you don't count the really big ones in New York City. And Mme Noelle is known throughout the ballet community as an excellent teacher. I don't find her *quite* so intimidating anymore.

I looked up to see that Katie Beth Parsons had just finished her routine. She looked pretty happy with herself, but then she usually does. She's kind of one of Madame's pets — she has been since she was the youngest member of the class when she joined it. Now that I've joined, she isn't the youngest anymore (she's twelve), but she's still a favorite of Madame's.

"Nice work, Katie Beth," I said as she came off the stage.

She looked at me suspiciously. "Thanks,"

she said, as if she weren't sure whether or not I meant the compliment. Katie Beth and I have not always been the best of friends — in fact, there have been times when we were downright enemies — but we've been getting along pretty well lately. Still, the atmosphere at most auditions isn't the friendliest.

Katie Beth pulled at the elastic of her leotard as she stood next to me, watching the rest of the students complete the routine. "I hate this stupid thing," she said. "I wish we could wear whatever we wanted instead of these."

We were all wearing the exact same outfits: a black leotard with pink tights. It's kind of like the uniform for my class. I could just imagine the scene if we were allowed to wear anything: There'd be so much neon in the place that it would look like Times Square. I myself don't really mind having to wear the same thing to each class — in fact, it's good to have one less thing to decide on as I pack my dance bag.

And it's not as if we can't express our individuality. There's room for that in how we each decide to do our hair. The only requirement is that it be "off zee face," as Mme Noelle puts it. I like to wrap mine into a tight bun or to braid it. Carrie usually has some kind of ponytail on the side of her head. And Hilary — well, Hilary's a whole different story.

Hilary Morgan always has the best of everything. A brand-new leotard every few weeks. New toe shoes as often as she needs them. (The rest of us have to make them last — toe shoes are awfully expensive.) And she doesn't do her own hair — she gets it "done" in a very fancy French braid a few times a week.

It's not that Hilary's family is all that rich (although they're certainly not poor). It's just that Hilary's career as a dancer is top priority with her mom. See, Mrs. Morgan used to be a ballet dancer herself, but she gave up her career to have a family. As I understand it (from what I've overheard in the dressing room) she's one of the worst "stage mothers" in the history of the school. She really *pushes* Hilary all the time; I know because I've seen her do it. She actually sits and watches our entire two-hour class sometimes!

Luckily, she wasn't watching that day — we didn't need any distractions. I don't think Mme Noelle would have tolerated a visitor during auditions anyway.

All of a sudden, I noticed that the last dancers had finished. Auditions were over. Mme Noelle called us all out onto the stage. She looked us up and down without saying a word. Then she smiled.

"All of my mademoiselles have done very, very well today," she said. "But only one can be zee Princess Aurora." Suddenly she clapped her hands three times. "Go now!" she said. "Change zee clothes. When you are ready, come back. I will give my decision zen."

We all scurried into the dressing room and raced to be the first out of our leotards. Everybody was talking at once, asking the others how they'd looked as they performed.

"Did you notice when I shook on the *arabesque*?" asked Lisa Jones, as she pulled on an oversized sweat shirt. I like Lisa, but sometimes she worries too much about her performance in class.

I shook my head. "Sorry, but I wasn't paying that much attention," I said. "I think I was on Mars for awhile there." That's what it had felt like — I'd been concentrating so hard that I felt like I'd been on a different planet.

"I thought I'd die by the time I *bourrée*'d across that whole huge stage," said Hilary. "It's not fair that the stage is so much bigger than our usual studio."

"Sure it's fair," said Carrie. "We all have to do the same thing on the same stage, don't we?"

"I guess," said Hilary. But she didn't sound convinced.

I stuffed my leotard and tights into my dance bag, and then carefully wrapped the ribbons around my toe shoes and laid them on top.

You have to take very good care of them, otherwise they won't last.

"I just hope Madame noticed how much I've been working on my arm movements," said Carrie. She stuffed her toe shoes into her bag, got up, and left the dressing room.

"Actually, she better hope that Madame *didn't* notice she's completely over the hill," said Hilary, giggling.

Over the hill! It was true that Carrie was one of the oldest students in class, but really! She's only a few years older than me! Ballet may *look* like a graceful, dainty world — but it's not. It's as tough and competitive as any sport. I could have spoken up in Carrie's defense, but I held my tongue. I don't like to get into any of the gossip and backbiting that often goes on in the dressing room.

Hilary looked in the mirror and patted her still perfectly braided hair. "I'm just dying to dance Princess Aurora," she said. "What a great part." Then she spun on her heel and headed out of the room.

"The rest of us just better pray that she doesn't get that part," said Katie Beth. "If she does, we'll have to put up with Mrs. Morgan practically sitting in our laps during every rehearsal!"

"I know," said Lisa. "I think Hilary's mom would dance the part *for* her, if she could."

9

I shook my head and kept quiet. Everybody was being pretty catty that day. I guess the auditions brought it out.

Finally we were all finished changing. We sat in a semicircle on the floor of the dance studio, facing Mme Noelle. She was seated on a chair, and she looked very serious.

"*Zee Sleeping Beauty* is one of zee most beautiful ballets in zee world," she began. "To perform in it is a privilege, no matter how small zee role."

Right. But none of us wanted "zee small roles." We all wanted the lead.

"To begin," said Mme Noelle, "zee part of zee Lilac Fairy will be donced by Lisa Jones."

Lisa smiled. I don't think she had really expected to get the lead. The Lilac Fairy is a pretty good role, and she looked happy to get it.

"Next," said Mme Noelle, "zee part of zee Bluebird of Happiness." That part is usually played by a man, but it sounded like someone from our class would be playing it instead. There aren't too many boys in the school — and there are none in our class. "Zis will be donced by Carrie Steinfeld."

Carrie let out a breath, then pressed her lips together and tried to smile at Mme Noelle. "Thank you," she said. "I know that the Bluebird's *pas de deux* is famous. I will try to do it justice."

I had to hand it to her — she handled the disappointment well.

"And now," said Mme Noelle, "I will tell zee news you are all waiting for." She paused. "Zere is only one student in zis class who has zee talent and zee *je ne sais quois* to bring zee role of Princess Aurora to life."

Zhuh-nuh-seh-kwah? What on earth did *that* mean? I'd never heard the expression before.

"Zat student is Mademoiselle Romsey," finished Mme Noelle.

I was still trying to figure out what she meant, and I didn't really hear my name. The next thing I knew, Lisa was giving me a quick hug. "All right, Jessi," she said. "You did it again!" She seemed genuinely happy for me.

"Congratulations," said Katie Beth sort of halfheartedly. I smiled vaguely. It still hadn't sunk in that I had won the role. That meant that I had gotten yet *another* lead in a production! I'd loved dancing in *Swan Lake*. And playing Swanilda in *Coppélia* had been pretty incredible. But the Princess Aurora! It was the role of a lifetime.

When I finally came to my senses, I was alone in the room. Except for Mme Noelle. She was smiling gently at me. "Congratulations, Jessica," she said. "You earned zee part."

"Thank you, Madame," I said, blushing. "But there's one thing I want to know. What does 'zhuh-nuh-seh-kwah' *mean?*"

"It simply means 'zat certain something' — zat indescribable feeling," she answered. "And you, my mademoiselle, possess it."

I blushed again. Then I thanked her once more, said good-bye, and ran out to wait for my ride home.

Hilary Morgan's mother pulled up just as I reached the outside stairs, where we all wait for our parents. Hilary started to walk toward the car, looking like she was headed for a funeral.

"Did you get the lead?" called Mrs. Morgan loudly.

Hilary shook her head. I saw Mrs. Morgan frown and heard her start to lecture as Hilary got into the car. "Didn't I *tell* you . . ." she began.

I turned away — I just couldn't listen to any more. Part of me almost wished that Hilary had gotten the part. Poor Hilary. But — I have to admit it — a bigger part of me was so happy I could hardly stand it. "Princess Aurora," I said to myself softly. "Princess Aurora."

CHAPTER 2

After Hilary left, I sat down to wait for my dad. I was still in a state of shock about getting the lead, but I thought that — just for fun — I'd play it cool with him.

Pretty soon, Daddy pulled up in front of the steps. I opened the car door and slid in, throwing my dance bag onto the backseat.

"Hi, baby!" he said, giving me a kiss. He started the car, and I saw him looking at me out of the corner of his eye as he pulled into traffic. He was being careful not to be pushy — but I could tell he was dying to know how the auditions had gone. "How did it go?" he asked casually.

"Pretty well," I answered, just as casually. "I mean, okay, I guess." I was bursting with my news, but I guess I also just felt like holding it in for a little while.

We'd only gone about three blocks before I

couldn't stand it anymore. "Daddy!" I said. "I did it! I'm Aurora!"

He turned to grin at me. "All right!" he said, holding up his hand for a high five. "I knew you could do it." A horn honked, and Daddy straightened out the car.

"I want to hear all about it," he said, "but let's wait till we're home, so you can tell everybody all at once." Then he pulled the car over to the curb and turned off the engine. "Wait here," he said. "I'm going to run into the store for some ice cream. We've got something to celebrate tonight!"

The minute we pulled into our driveway, Becca came running out of the front door. "Did you get a part?" she asked excitedly. Mama was right behind her, carrying Squirt. Aunt Cecelia stood in the doorway, holding a dishcloth.

Becca is my little sister. She's eight and a half, and she's a pretty great kid, even if she does drive me up the wall sometimes. She's really bright, and she has a great imagination. Becca loves to come and see me in my productions. In fact, she'd probably like to be in one herself — except for one thing. Becca has the worst case of stage fright I've ever seen.

Squirt, who was now looking at me and saying, "Buh!" with a big smile on his face, is just a toddler. Squirt's not his real name, of course. His real name is John Philip Ramsey, Jr. — but Squirt suits him much better. He was named that by the nurses at the hospital where he was born, because he was the smallest baby there. He only weighed five pounds, eight ounces back then! Now he's a big lug — a big, squirmy lug, who was doing his best to get out of Mama's arms.

"I'll take him," I said. "C'mere, Squirtman." I took him from Mama and balanced him on my hip. I smiled at him. "How does it feel to be carried by a princess?" I asked.

Mama gasped. "You got the role?" she asked.

"Yup," I answered. "Princess Aurora, at your service."

Becca was all over me, shrieking and smacking my arm.

"Okay, Becca," said Aunt Cecelia. "Let's let the princess come in and have her dinner." Aunt Cecelia likes to try to keep things calm. She's Daddy's older sister, and she came to live with us not long ago, when Mama decided to go back to work and realized she'd need help with Squirt in order to do that.

At first, having Aunt Cecelia live with us seemed like a big mistake. Becca and I thought she was too strict and too mean. She treated us like babies. But she learned to give us some credit for being able to take care of ourselves — and we learned to like her better. Now we're glad she's here.

At dinner, I filled my family in on the details of the audition. And over ice cream (I had a tiny bit, even though I really have to watch what I eat, especially when we're preparing a performance) I told them all about *The Sleeping Beauty*.

"You all know the story," I said. "It's just like the fairy tale. It starts with the christening of the baby Princess Aurora. All the fairies do beautiful dances as they present their gifts."

"Then the bad fairy comes, right?" asked Becca.

"That's right. The funny thing is that the bad fairy is usually played by a man in a wig," I said. "Anyway, the bad fairy puts a curse on the baby, telling her that she will prick her finger and die on her sixteenth birthday. A good fairy, called the Lilac Fairy, can't get rid of the curse. But she at least makes it so that Aurora will sleep for a hundred years instead of die."

"Then what happens?" asked Daddy. I guess he doesn't remember fairy tales as well as the rest of us.

"Well, I come on stage in the next act, which is my sixteenth birthday party. Four princes present me with roses, and I do this gorgeous slow dance called the 'Rose Adagio.' It's really hard. Then the bad witch, in disguise, sneaks into the party and hands me a spindle for making yarn and I prick my finger on it and fall into a deep sleep.

"A hundred years later," I went on, "this prince is looking for me. He sees a vision of me — which is really me, of course — and we dance together. Then the prince tries to find me, and when he finally does, he kisses me — "

"Ew!" interrupted Becca. "Do you really have to kiss a boy? I'd rather kiss Misty any day!" Misty is our pet hamster.

I ignored her. " — and I wake up, and then there's the wedding, where I dance with all these different fairy-tale characters, like the Bluebird of Happiness. I don't really know what that has to do with the plot, but it's a great dance. And then I dance with the prince again at the very end." I was exhausted just thinking about it.

"It sounds like a beautiful ballet," said Mama.

"It is," I said. "And you should hear the music. It's by Tchaikovsky, the same composer who wrote the music for *Swan Lake*."

After dinner, I headed upstairs (Mama said I could be excused from table clearing and dish washing, since it was a special night) to call Mallory. I couldn't wait to tell her my news, and I knew she'd spread it around to our friends.

Who is Mallory? Maybe I should tell you about her — and about my other friends, too.

Mallory Pike is my best friend, and the first friend I made when my family moved to Stoneybrook. She's terrific. She's smart and funny, and we have great times together. We both love to read — especially horse stories, like *Misty of Chincoteague* — but Mal also likes to write. Someday she hopes to be a writer and illustrator of children's books, which I think is a neat idea.

Part of what makes Mallory fun is that she's easygoing and doesn't get fazed by much. I think that's because she comes from a huge — and I mean huge — family. Mallory is eleven like me, and she has seven little brothers and sisters! Three of them are triplets, believe it or not. Their names are Adam, Jordan, and Byron, and they're ten. Then comes Vanessa — she's nine — and Nicky, who's eight, followed by Margo, who's seven. The baby of the family is Claire. She's five. The Pike household is never boring. Actually, I think that Mal sometimes envies my (relatively) quiet family. She doesn't get much private time.

Even though she's the oldest, Mallory feels that her parents still treat her like a kid. (I can relate to that!) She had to work really hard on her parents — just like I did — to convince them to let her get her ears pierced. Her next project is to get contacts, but I think that's a long way off. With her red hair and freckles, and her glasses and her braces, Mal has a hard time feeling glamorous — even with pierced ears. But you know what? I bet she's going to be a real knockout someday. She just has to be patient. (I should talk. I'm as impatient as she is.)

When I first moved to Stoneybrook, I felt so lonely. I'd just left my best friend, Keisha (who also happens to be my cousin), and I wondered if I'd ever find another best friend. But as it turned out, I not only found Mallory, which was great, but a whole bunch of other friends. These friends are all very different from each other, but they have one thing in common. They love baby-sitting, just like I do. And that's why they formed the Baby-sitters Club. I'm lucky to be a member and to have them all as friends. Mallory and I are the youngest in the club, by the way. Everyone else is thirteen.

Kristy Thomas is the president of the BSC. She's something else. When I first met Kristy, I was a little intimidated — she's very straight-forward (sometimes she's even got a big mouth) and energetic. But now I like her, and admire her, a lot. She's always having these great ideas — and she acts on them, too. She's not just a dreamer.

Kristy's family is pretty complicated to describe, but here goes. First of all, her parents got divorced years ago after her dad walked out, leaving Kristy's mom to take care of Kristy and her brothers. (She's got two older brothers, Charlie and Sam, and a younger one named David Michael.) Mrs. Thomas did a good job of being a single parent. But then she met Watson Brewer, who is a real, true millionaire. They fell in love and got married, and Kristy and her family moved across town to live in Watson's mansion.

But it's not just the six of them in that gigantic house. Watson had also been married before, and he has two kids — Karen (she's seven) and Andrew (he's four). They stay with the Brewers and Thomases every other weekend and for two weeks in the summer. Karen and Andrew love Kristy, and she loves them, too. No wicked stepfamilies here!

You'd think that a family that size would be enough. But you'd be wrong. Kristy's mom and Watson recently decided to adopt Emily Michelle, this two-and-a-half-year-old Vietnamese girl. (She's an absolute doll!) And then Nannie, Kristy's grandmother, moved in to help take care of Emily. Wow. Now that's a big family. And I haven't even told you about

Shannon and Boo-Boo. (Don't worry, they're not more kids. Shannon's a dog and Boo-Boo's a cat.) Plus, there are some goldfish.

So that's Kristy. Oh! I forgot to tell you what she looks like. Kristy is on the short side, and she's got brown hair and brown eyes. And she's kind of a tomboy — that is, she doesn't care much about clothes or makeup, she likes to play baseball, and she's not all that interested in boys.

Kristy's best friend (I think they've been best friends all their lives) is Mary Anne Spier. She and Kristy look alike, with their brown hair and brown eyes (although Mary Anne cares a little more about clothes), but other than that they are very different. You've heard the saying "opposites attract"? That describes Mary Anne and Kristy. While Kristy is assertive and loudmouthed, Mary Anne is very quiet and shy, and incredibly sensitive.

I'm not sure why she is that way, but sometimes I think it may have to do with the way she grew up. Mary Anne's mother died when Mary Anne was tiny, and so her dad was the one who brought her up. I've heard that he used to be very strict with her — but he seems to be pretty loose now. He even dealt well with the fact that Mary Anne had a steady boyfriend for awhile (she's the only one of us club members who did). I guess it helped that he likes Logan. (That's Logan Bruno, Mary Anne's ex-boyfriend. He's in the club, too, actually — but I'll tell you about that later.)

Maybe part of what loosened up Mr. Spier was falling in love and getting married again. Now, that's a romantic story. He met up with an old girlfriend from high school, started to date her again, and then he married her. And the best part of the story is that the old girlfriend happens to be Dawn Schafer's mother! Who is Dawn Schafer?

Dawn is another member of the club, and she's not only Mary Anne's stepsister; she's her best friend, too. (That's right, Mary Anne has two best friends.) Dawn's mom grew up in Stoneybrook but then moved to California, got married, and had two kids — Dawn and her younger brother, Jeff. But then she got divorced and moved back to Stoneybrook — a fact for which we are all thankful, since that move brought us Dawn. The only bad part about the move was that Jeff missed California and his dad so much that he ended up moving back there to live. So her family's split up, but Dawn handles it well.

Dawn is truly gorgeous. She's got incredibly long, white-blonde hair and she dresses in a style all her own. She wears all these great, casual clothes in bright colors. Nobody else in

Stoneybrook dresses like that — you could pick Dawn out as a California girl in a minute. She's different in other ways, too: She loves the sun and the sea, and she adores health food. Bean sprouts are to Dawn what Ho-Ho's are to Claudia.

Claudia — that's Claudia Kishi, the vice-president of the BSC — is the Junk Food Queen. I've never seen anyone eat the way she does and still have such a great figure and perfect skin. I don't know how she does it, but Claudia always looks great. She has an incredible sense of style. She's also a great artist, which might have something to do with it.

Claudia is Japanese-American and very exotic-looking. She's got this long, silky black hair that she wears in a million different ways, and gorgeous almond-shaped eyes. Her family is pretty small — there's just her and her sister, Janine (who is a real — I swear it — genius), and their parents. Claudia's grandmother Mimi used to live with them, but she died not long ago. I get the feeling that Claud still misses Mimi all the time; they were very, very close.

Unlike her genius sister, Claudia is not a great student. It's not that she's dumb, but there are other things she'd rather do with her time than study — like sculpt or paint or make collages. She'd also like to spend her time munching on junk food while reading Nancy Drew books, but there's a limit to how much of that she can do, especially since her parents disapprove of both activities. Which is why you never know when you're in Claudia's room where you might find a Devil Dog or a Twinkie or a Three Musketeers. She hides them. Everywhere. Just like she hides her Nancy Drew books.

But even though Claudia's parents are strict about some things, they're pretty easy about others. Like clothes. Mallory and I are always fighting with our parents for the right to wear certain things — like miniskirts or big T-shirts over leggings. But Claudia's parents seem to let her wear whatever she wants. I think they see her outfits as part of her artistic expression. (I'm so jealous!)

Stacey McGill is a really cool dresser, too. In fact, I think that's why she and Claudia became best friends at first. And one of the reasons Stacey's a sophisticated dresser is that she grew up in New York City. That's right, New York City — home of some of the best ballet companies in the world, not to mention the greatest restaurants, dance clubs, department stores . . .

But Stacey likes Stoneybrook. She first came here when her dad was transferred to Stamford, but then she actually moved back to New York when he was transferred again. The rest of the club members thought they'd lost Stacey forever. But then they heard bad news and good news. The bad news was that Stacey's parents were getting a divorce. The good news was that she and her mom were moving to Stoneybrook again!

Unfortunately, they couldn't move into their old house. Why? Because my family had moved into it in the meantime! They did find another nice house, though, and of course Stacey was back in the club right away.

Stacey's very cool, as you might expect her to be. She gets her blonde hair permed every now and then, and as I said before, she rivals Claudia for "Trendiest Dresser in Stoneybrook."

There's one other thing about Stacey — she's a diabetic. That means she has to take really good care of herself, watch her diet like a hawk, and (I could never do this!) give herself daily injections of insulin. Stacey doesn't seem to let it get to her, though — she's usually in a great mood.

Speaking of great moods, that night I was in about the best mood possible. The time right after you learn that you've won a great part is always the best — before the hard work of rehearsal begins. As I passed the hall mirror on my way to call Mallory, I gave myself a big smile. "Hey, Aurora!" I said. "What's new?"

CHAPTER 3

"*Love* your leg warmers, Lisa," said Carrie. "Are they new?"

We were all in the dressing room, getting ready for our first day of rehearsals for *The Sleeping Beauty*. I was still pretty excited about being chosen to play Princess Aurora, but I knew enough to keep my mouth shut. Most of my classmates were probably happy for me, but nobody likes a gloating prima ballerina.

"They really are great, Lisa," I said. "Where'd you get them?"

"My mom got them in the city," she answered. "At Capezio's. She gave them to me last night. They're lilac, because I'm playing the Lilac Fairy."

Lisa seemed happy with her role, and I was glad. I have this weird thing sometimes, where even though I'm thrilled to get the lead, I kind of feel bad about it, too. Because if I got it, that means that somebody else didn't. Does that make any sense?

I threw my dance bag down next to my locker and started to change. It seems like I'm always in a hurry in the dressing room, but so is everybody else. There's this feeling that Mme Noelle is waiting for us in the studio, getting more and more impatient by the minute. And having Mme Noelle in a bad mood is bad news.

I threw off my school clothes (jeans, a new red sweater, and my red high-tops) and stuffed them into my locker. It's never a good idea to put things on the benches in the dressing room, even for a minute. They'd get all mixed up with everybody *else's* stuff and there would be mass confusion.

Then I groped around in my dance bag and pulled out my leotard and tights. I shimmied into them in about three seconds (after years of practice) and then reached for my toe shoes. I could put them on in the studio while I was listening to Mme Noelle give us the rehearsal schedule.

My toe shoes weren't in the bag.

I checked again. No toe shoes. My red high-tops were in there, but no toe shoes. Now, you have to understand that I have been dancing for seven years. For at least the last four I have packed my own dance bag. And I have never, *ever* once forgotten anything. Other girls would have to dance with bare legs when they forgot their tights, or in old bathing suits when they'd left their leotards at home. Not me. Never. I was always prepared. It's just the way I am.

"Mademoiselles!" called Mme Noelle from outside the dressing room. "Are we plonning to donce today?" She clapped her hands loudly, just once. That meant, in Madame's special shorthand, "Get into the studio, NOW!"

I panicked. I bent over my dance bag and practically turned it inside out. They *had* to be in there! I clearly remembered putting them in the bag the night before, after they'd aired out enough so that they'd be ready to wear again.

I looked around the dressing room. There were heaps of clothing everywhere — tangled leg warmers on the benches, leotards hanging by one sleeve from a locker door — but not a toe shoe in sight. What was I going to do?

Everybody else was hurrying out of the dressing room. Mary stopped for a moment as she passed my locker.

"What's the matter, Jessi?" she asked.

I told her that my toe shoes were missing. Her eyes grew round. She knew how serious this was.

"I wish I could lend you a pair, but my spare ones are at home," she said.

"That's okay," I said. "I really couldn't dance in anyone else's shoes anyway." My toe shoes are unique — everybody's are. And every dancer has a different way of taking care of them. There's a whole routine with toe shoes — you have to break them in (I do it by banging them against the banister on the staircase at home), and sew ribbons onto them, and stuff the toes with lambswool. So even though they don't last too long (I usually need a new pair every week or so), each pair has a lot of time invested in it. And each pair ends up fitting your feet, and your feet alone.

I do, of course, have a spare pair of toe shoes. But guess where they were. Right — they were at home.

"This is terrible," I said. By then I was alone in the dressing room. I could hear Mme Noelle's voice, just faintly. She was taking the roll in the studio. In about three seconds she'd realize that I wasn't there.

I was going to have to go into the studio barefoot.

I took a deep breath and started to walk. I stopped at the dressing room door and took one last look around the room. There was not a single toe shoe anywhere. I looked down at my feet. This was going to be humiliating. And

Mme Noelle wasn't going to like it at all.

At least my entrance was quiet. Bare feet make a lot less noise than toe shoes, which tend to make clunking noises when you try to walk normally.

But, as quiet as I was, everybody, including Mme Noelle, looked at me as I walked into the studio.

"Ah," said Madame. "Zee Princess Aurora hos decided to join us." She gestured to a spot on the floor. "Please, your highness, take a seat."

Then she saw my feet.

"But where are your shoes, Mademoiselle Romsey?" she asked, her eyebrows raised high.

I felt so ashamed. "I — I don't know," I said. "I packed them last night, but now they're not in my bag." I felt hot, then suddenly cold, all over.

"But you cannot rehearse wizout zem!" she said. "And we cannot rehearse wizout you." She stood up. "You must look for zem again. Perhops zey are benease some ozair girl's clothes. Come!" She clapped her hands and gestured to the class to follow her.

I felt like such a jerk, walking back into the dressing room with my entire class marching behind me. When we got there, we started to tear the place apart. Mme Noelle stood at the door of the room as we searched. She had a funny look on her face, as if she smelled a dead fish or something. Usually, she made a point of staying out of the dressing room — and it was obvious that she wasn't enjoying this little visit.

"What is *zot*?" she asked, pointing at Carrie's neon green, pink, and yellow jacket, which was tossed over a sink.

"That's my jacket," said Carrie.

"I see," sniffed Mme Noelle.

"I think it's wicked cool," said Katie Beth. "I wish I had one."

"Perhops if you young ladies were more careful with your sings, zis would not hoppen," said Mme Noelle, looking at me.

I felt tears stinging my eyes. It wasn't fair! True, everybody's stuff was strewn all over the room. But I'm actually a pretty neat person. *My* stuff is usually put away in my locker. And I'm always prepared for class. At least I always *have* been.

I looked around at my classmates. They'd finished poking through the piles of stuff and were looking back at me. I picked up my dance bag one more time and checked it again. No luck. It was empty, except for my high-tops. Too bad I couldn't dance in those.

I looked at Mme Noelle and shrugged my

shoulders. "I'm sorry," I said. "They're not here."

She gave me a glance that said, as clearly as words would have, "Jessica Romsey, I am most disappointed in you." Then, out loud, she simply said, "Come."

We trooped back into the studio and got ready to warm up at the *barre*. I was just going to have to do the exercises barefoot. Mme Noelle put on some music and led us through a few minutes of *pliés* (plee-ay — that's when you sink down, keeping your backside tucked in and only bending at the knee) and *relevés* (reh-leh-vays — that's when you go up on your toes).

I saw her look at me as I *relevé'd*. Everybody else was *en pointe* — that is, *really* up on their toes. I was kind of just pretending. Madame shook her head, her lips in a tight line.

"Zis will not do," she said suddenly. "If Mademoiselle Romsey cannot practice *en pointe*, zere is no reason to rehearse today. After all, she is zee Princess Aurora, and we cannot do very much wizout her." She turned her back on us and lifted the needle from the record. "Zis rehearsal is concelled."

I was shocked. This was worse than I ever could have imagined! Everybody groaned. I knew how they felt. There's nothing worse than missing a day of dancing — it throws off your whole routine. And we needed every rehearsal that was scheduled. The performance wasn't all that far off.

"Isn't there any way we can still rehearse?" asked Lisa.

"What if we just look for the shoes one more time?" asked Hilary. "If Jessi says she brought them, they *must* be in that room somewhere."

Mme Noelle didn't look happy about the idea, but she agreed. "One more time," she said. "But zen, rehearsal is off."

I *hated* having her mad at me.

We all paraded back into the dressing room. I brought up the rear — I wasn't too enthusiastic about another pointless search. Just as I entered the room, I heard Katie Beth squeal.

"Hey, *here* they are," she said, holding up a pair of toe shoes. They were mine. I could tell from across the room. "They were in your bag the whole time, Jessi."

I ran over to her and grabbed them without even saying thanks. My shoes! I'd never been so happy to see them. But I knew Katie Beth was wrong. Those shoes had definitely *not* been in my bag the whole time. I knew it as surely as I knew my own name.

"Very good, Katie Beth," said Madame. "Zee mystery is solved. Now let us get on wiz zee rehearsal!"

She led us back into the studio and the rehearsal began for real. I put on my toe shoes as Madame told us about the first part of the dance we would be practicing.

"And zen," she said, "zee Princess Aurora enters wiz a *glissade* . . ." She made a movement that suggested what I was supposed to do. ". . . and zen a *relevé en arabesque*." Again, she illustrated what she meant.

I love to watch Mme Noelle move. She doesn't dress in leotards for class — she just wears a turtleneck and a long black skirt. And when she demonstrates steps, she doesn't do them full out. But every move she makes is just so — so full of grace is the only way I can describe it. You can see all those years of dance training in the slightest motion of her arm. I don't think she knows *how* to move like a regular person anymore. I wonder if I'll ever have that kind of poise.

For me, for now, ballet is more like hard work. The stuff I do without having to think about is stuff I've been doing nearly every day for seven years. And everything new I learn is based on those foundations. It takes a long, long time to learn to dance.

I tried to concentrate on learning my steps. I was doing the best I could to forget about the whole miserable scene before rehearsal. But I couldn't get it out of my head.

Mme Noelle couldn't either — that was obvious. She was very impatient with me, and since I was feeling distracted, she kept having to repeat directions. That didn't help.

"Long neck, Mademoiselle Romsey!" she said. "You are not doncing zee part of a hunchback. You are a princess — please act like one."

I stretched my neck and proceeded to stumble in the middle of my *glissade*. I heard somebody giggle behind me. Wonderful! I just knew that everybody in the class was now convinced that I was a complete airhead. Once again I tried to concentrate.

"STEP!" said Mme Noelle suddenly, clapping her hands. I had gotten off the beat. This was just not my day. She went to the record player and started the music from the beginning. "And . . . again," she said, nodding at me. "I want nossing but grace from all of you," she said. "I want absolutely magnificent, glorious grace."

Right.

I worked harder and harder, forgetting the time, forgetting my lost shoes, forgetting everything except the music and how I was moving to it.

Before I knew it, Mme Noelle was clapping her hands. "Okay, mademoiselles," she said. "Next time we will do better, am I right?"

I met her eyes and nodded. She gave me a tight smile — I guess she was going to forgive me.

I walked to the dressing room, relieved that rehearsal was finally over. I changed back into my school clothes and reached into my dance bag for my high-tops. I was thinking that the next rehearsal would just *have* to go better than this one — it certainly couldn't go any worse. Then I pulled my left sneaker out of the bag and saw something stuck between the laces.

It was a note. And this is what it said: BEWARE. Nothing more, nothing less. Just . . . BEWARE.

I couldn't figure out what it was supposed to mean. Beware of what? Beware of whom? I thought it was pretty strange. But I was too tired from rehearsal to wonder about it for long. I shoved it into my bag and headed out the door.

CHAPTER 4

I was still feeling a little shaky by the time I got to Claudia's for that day's Baby-sitters Club meeting, but I tried not to let it show as I slipped into my regular spot next to Mallory on the floor. As usual, I had arrived about two and a half seconds before Kristy called the meeting to order. (I nearly always get there just under the wire because of dance class, but nobody gives me a hard time about it, which I'm thankful for.)

I guess I forgot to mention that our club always meets at Claudia's house, in her room. This is why: Claudia, the vice-president of the club, has her own phone and her own personal phone number. That means that we're not tying up any adult's phone while we take calls during meetings.

Let me go back and explain a little bit about how the club began and how it works. The whole thing was Kristy's idea originally. Remember how I told you that she's always having good ideas? Well, this was the ultimate good idea, and here's how it happened: One afternoon, way back before Kristy's mom married Watson Brewer, David Michael needed a baby-sitter. Usually Kristy or her brothers would have watched him, but this time none of them could. Mrs. Thomas made about three zillion phone calls looking for a sitter, but she wasn't having any luck.

That's when Kristy had her brainstorm. What if parents could reach a whole crew of sitters, just by making one phone call? It seemed like a great idea. Kristy talked to her two friends Mary Anne and Claudia (who were interested) and they started a club — The Baby-sitters Club (or the BSC). Three people didn't seem like enough for a club, though, so Claudia asked Stacey, whom she was becoming friends with to join. It was just the four of them until Dawn moved to town and became friends with Mary Anne. Dawn had done some baby-sitting out in California, so they asked her to be a member, too.

Mallory and I joined the BSC during the time that Stacey was back in New York, before her parents got divorced. The rest of the club members were feeling kind of overwhelmed with jobs, and we were available, so it worked out for everyone. Even though (we think) we're lowly sixth-graders and can only sit during the day (except for our own families), I think we fit in pretty well.

So, all together there are seven of us now, and it seems like the club is just the right size. In fact, I don't think Claudia's room could hold too many more people without bursting at the seams.

The way the club works is pretty simple. We meet on Mondays, Wednesdays, and Fridays from 5:30 to 6:00. Parents can call during those times to arrange for a sitter. (Most of the parents have been using us forever; new clients find out about us through the fliers we distribute from time to time, or by word of mouth.)

Kristy is the club president, and she takes her job pretty seriously: She's all business at meetings. She always sits in Claudia's director's chair, with a visor on her head and a pencil over her ear. She calls each meeting to order just as the digital clock flips to 5:30. Sometimes she asks us if we've read the club notebook. (We always say yes, because we always have.)

The club notebook, in case you're wondering, is the place where we record every job we go on. We write down what happened, who it happened to, why it happened, and anything else we can think of. Seriously, it's a good thing that we have it. Reading it keeps us up to date on our clients and what's going on with them. The only thing is, it's kind of time consuming to write all that stuff down — and then to read what everybody else wrote. But it's worth it. By the way, the notebook was Kristy's idea (of course).

Anyway, let's get back to answering the phone. When a call comes in, someone takes it (we all dive for it) and finds out when and where the job will be. Then we tell the parent that we'll call right back. Next, Mary Anne, the club secretary, checks the record book. (It's different from the notebook.)

The record book is kind of an amazing thing. In it, Mary Anne keeps track of all our schedules: Claudia's art classes, my dance classes and rehearsals, Mal's orthodontist appointments . . . you get the idea. Then, when a call comes in, she only needs to take a quick peek to see which of us is free. In the record book is a lot of other stuff besides our schedules. It has records about all our clients: names, addresses, phone numbers — and also stuff about the kids we sit for, like who's allergic to what.

Anyway, once Mary Anne finds out who's free, it's usually a simple matter to decide which of those sitters gets the job. We rarely squabble over jobs, since there's always enough work to go around. Then we call back the parent and confirm the job. And that's it!

Well, not quite. I forgot to tell you about the treasury. Stacey, the math genius, is in charge of that. As treasurer, she can tell you in about three seconds exactly how much money we have available.

Where does the money come from? Well, it's like this. We keep all the money we earn on jobs — that's ours. But every Monday, we pay club dues. (Not without a lot of complaining, I might add — we hate to part with our hard-earned money.) The dues are used for club stuff, like paying Kristy's brother Charlie to drive her back and forth to meetings since she lives too far away to walk now.

We also use the money for the occasional pizza bash or for sleepover munchies. (We're not all business, all the time!) And we use some of it for supplies for our Kid-Kits. Kid-Kits are yet another of Kristy's great ideas. They're really just cardboard boxes, but we've each decorated our own with all kinds of stickers and sequins and stuff. The boxes are stocked with things that kids love — crayons and books and puzzles and paper dolls . . . stuff like that. We bring them on any job where they might come in handy.

Okay, so Kristy is the president, Claudia is

vice-president, Mary Anne is secretary, and Stacey is treasurer. You might be wondering where that leaves Dawn, Mallory, and me. Well, Dawn is what we call an alternate officer. That means that any time one of the others can't make it to the meeting, Dawn fills in for them. She has to know how to do everyone else's job.

Mallory and I are junior officers, which really doesn't mean much at all, except that we're younger and that we can only sit during the afternoons. This is fine with me — I don't know if I'm really ready to sit in some strange house alone at night! (I do sit for my own brother and sister at night, and Mal sits at her house — but that's different.)

There are also two other members whom I haven't told you about. They're associate members, and they don't come to meetings. But they do take jobs, when the rest of us are all booked up — and that's been a big help more than once. Logan Bruno, Mary Anne's ex-boyfriend, is one of the associate members. (He's really nice — and you should hear his neat Southern accent. He moved to Stoney-brook from Louisville, Kentucky, and he sounds like someone out of *Gone With the Wind*. He and Mary Anne are still good friends, by the way.) The other associate member is Shannon Kilbourne, this girl who lives in Kristy's new neighborhood. I don't know her too well, but she seems nice.

So there I was, sitting by Mallory on the floor of Claudia's room, ready for the meeting to start. Claudia, Mary Anne, and Dawn were all sitting cross-legged on the bed. Kristy was in the director's chair, and Stacey was sitting in Claudia's desk chair, leaning way back in it. She looked like she was about to topple over any minute.

"Did you see that outfit Jennifer Cooke had on today? I mean, she looked like a cross between Princess Di and Minnie Mouse!" said Claud all of a sudden.

That was all it took to make Stacey — and the chair — fall over. Stacey was fine. She just lay there on the floor, laughing until she was almost crying. "Who does she think she is, anyway — just because she's won some beauty pageants. All that makeup — it's too much!"

I was giggling, trying to imagine the outfit Claudia had described, when Kristy spoke up. "Order!" she said. It was 5:30. And our meetings *always* start on time.

Stacey got up from the floor and brushed off her jeans. She was wiping the tears from her eyes and trying to stifle her laughter. Kristy gave her a Look, which meant straighten up, but Stacey was too far gone. You know how it is when you're not *supposed* to be laughing — like in the library, or during science class — but you can't stop? That's how Stacey was.

She just kept shaking her head and saying "Minnie Mouse" and then breaking into giggles all over again. Kristy looked a little annoyed.

Luckily for Stacey, the phone rang then. Kristy dove for it. "Baby-sitters Club," she said, answering it. Then, "Sure, Mrs. Perkins. No problem. I'll call you right back." Kristy hung up and looked around the room. The phone call had given Stacey the chance to get serious. "Mrs. Perkins needs a sitter for Laura," said Kristy.

Laura is a baby. We usually sit for her *and* her two big sisters. "What about Myriah and Gabbie?" asked Mallory.

"The Perkinses are taking them to that big show in Stamford," said Kristy. "You know," she continued, "the one with Minnie Mouse on ice skates."

That did it. We all cracked up, including Kristy, and laughed until we were rolling on the floor. We didn't stop until the phone rang again.

We were busy handling calls and setting up jobs for awhile, so I had to wait for a chance to tell everybody about the disastrous rehearsal I'd had that afternoon. But finally there was a lull in the action, and I told the awful tale.

"Oh, Jessi!" said Mallory. "Did you just *die* of embarrassment when you had to come out barefoot? I would have."

I admitted that it had been pretty bad. "But the worst thing was that Madame Noelle was mad at me," I said.

Mary Anne smiled sympathetically. "You really care a lot about what she thinks of you, don't you?" she asked.

"I know how that is," said Claudia. "It's like if I don't finish a project in time for art class. I hate it when I let my teacher down."

"But it all worked out okay, right?" asked Dawn. "I mean, you found your toe shoes and everything. But I wonder about that note."

I nodded even though the note didn't have me all that worried. "It's just that I hate starting out a new production with a rehearsal like that," I said. Everybody was being so nice. There's nothing like supportive friends when you're feeling like a total loser. I noticed, though, that Kristy hadn't said anything. Maybe she just wasn't that interested in my ballet stories.

"Well, it's all over now," I said, getting ready to change the subject. I didn't want to make Kristy mad at me for taking up so much meeting time.

"Right, Jessi. Next time will be better," said Kristy quickly. "Now listen, you guys. I've got a great idea."

Everybody groaned, just to tease Kristy. How can anyone get so many great ideas all the time? No wonder she wasn't interested in my story — she'd been waiting impatiently the whole time, dying to tell us about her latest brainstorm.

"It seems to me that we haven't done anything really special with the kids we sit for lately," said Kristy. "You know, there hasn't been a big party, or a carnival, or anything — not for a long time."

"That's true," said Dawn. "But what can we do that would be new and exciting?"

"Are you ready for this?" asked Kristy, grinning. "We're going to have — a pet show!" She looked around the room. "I was remembering that Louie was in a pet show once," she continued. (Louie was this great collie that Kristy used to have. I never met him, though: He died before I moved here.) "It was at the library, and it was really fun. Louie won second prize! I was so proud of him."

Everybody loved Kristy's idea.

"The kids are going to think this is the greatest," said Mallory. "It'll be a chance to get

together and show off their pets. But where should we have it? We need lots of room."

"I was thinking it could be in Dawn and Mary Anne's backyard," said Kristy. "It's one of the biggest yards, and their house is pretty close to a lot of the kids' houses."

"Sounds great!" said Dawn. "I'm sure my mom won't mind."

"How are we going to let everyone know about this?" asked Stacey. "It's going to take a lot of planning."

"I'll make invitations," said Claudia. "We'll send them out to all our clients to let them know the time and place. We'd better pick a date a few weeks away, though — everybody's going to need time to get ready for this."

"We're also going to need prize ribbons, refreshments, and all kinds of other stuff," said Mary Anne. You could practically see the gears turning as she considered the details. She's a great organizer.

We worked on plans for the pet show for the rest of the meeting (between phone calls, that is). And I got so caught up in the whole thing that I almost forgot about my horrible rehearsal.

Almost.

CHAPTER 5

When the time came for the second rehearsal of *The Sleeping Beauty*, Princess Aurora was Princess Prepared. As I unpacked my dance bag in the dressing room, I almost had to laugh. I'd brought not just my spare toe shoes, but a spare dance outfit. The entire thing.

Two pairs of pink tights. Two black leotards. Two hair-ties (it wouldn't do to have my hair-tie disappear and have to dance with my hair in my face — Mme Noelle would be furious). Two pairs of leg warmers (one white, one purple) and two baggy old gray sweat shirts, for warm-ups. I wasn't taking any chances.

As I changed, I watched my stuff like a hawk. When I walked across the room to check my hair in the mirror, I kept looking over my shoulder to make sure nobody went near my bag. I must have looked pretty paranoid. But I didn't care. Knowing that I had everything

49

I needed for class made me feel safe. I was sure that everything would go smoothly that day.

"Coming, Jessi?" asked Katie Beth. "I see you brought your toe shoes this time."

I gritted my teeth. Sometimes Katie Beth can be really irritating. "For your information," I answered, "I brought them *last* time, too."

"Sure, Jessi," said Katie Beth. "Anything you say." She ran on ahead, into the studio. I walked behind her, giving her dirty looks.

"Why zee cloudy face, Mademoiselle Romsey?" asked Madame as I walked into the room.

I changed my frown to a smile, in a flash. "Good afternoon, Madame Noelle," I said, trying to sound happy. By then she was busy picking out the records for the day's practice, and she just nodded at me.

"All right, mademoiselles," she said. "Let us begin zee warm-up."

We took our places at the *barre* and began to work through the familiar exercises that I could probably do in my sleep. Sometimes I wonder just how many *pliés* I've done over the years, rising and falling to the sound of tinkly piano music.

When I was younger, taking beginner's classes, we used to play fun little games. For example, the teacher used to let us guess what the music was after each exercise. The records were always classical arrangements of simple songs like "Three Blind Mice," and we were very competitive about seeing who could guess right most often.

But games like that are out of the question now. Mme Noelle's class is serious. We don't giggle, we don't whisper, and we don't ask questions like, "What's fifth position, again?" But you know what? Even though the early days were fun, I like this ultraserious kind of class even better.

I like to work hard. I like to concentrate. And I love the fact that all the painstaking, repetitive work I do is worth it. You know why? Because it lets me fly. That's how I feel sometimes; when I'm in the middle of a *tour jeté* (toor jet-tay — that's just a big jump), I feel like I'm flying. And then it doesn't seem like work at all — it feels effortless, and graceful, and . . . just wonderful.

When we'd finished our warm-up, we left the *barre* and stood in the middle of the room, while Mme Noelle changed the record. Soon, Tchaikovsky's music filled the air. It was beautiful.

Madame stood in front of the room, working out the step she was about to teach us. She made motions with her hands, and whispered words like *glissade* and *pique* to herself. While

I waited for her to be ready, I looked into the big mirror that covered one wall of the studio.

I checked my posture. Good, but not good enough. I pulled up my head ("Like there is a string from the ceiling, holding you up," as Mme Noelle always says) and pulled in my stomach. I held out my right arm and arranged my hand as gracefully as I could. There! That looked good.

You might think that the other girls in class would think I was weird for looking at myself that way, but no. They were all doing it, too. Ballet students are always checking their form, because their form is important. You've got to be "just so," all the time.

"Mademoiselle Romsey," said Mme Noelle. "And Mademoiselle Steinfeld and Mademoiselle Jones. Attention, please."

She was ready to show us our steps. I paid close attention — you don't want to have to ask Mme Noelle to go over the steps more than once.

She gave us the whole routine in a flurry of French words. We followed along, practicing without doing the steps full out. Just as she was getting to the last *arabesque*, Carrie lost her balance, knocked into me, and fell down.

"Jessi, you klutz!" she said loudly.

Me? I couldn't believe it. I hadn't had anything to do with it! Carrie was the klutz, not me. I looked up at Mme Noelle and opened my mouth to defend myself. But when I saw the look she was giving me, I decided to forget it. She clearly had not forgotten the episode of the toe shoes, and I was better off just keeping quiet.

So instead of sticking up for myself, I helped Carrie to her feet. Did she thank me? Three guesses.

"Again, mademoiselles," said Madame, barely pausing for Carrie to catch her breath. "And *one*, two, three . . ."

We went back into the routine. I was fighting to regain the concentration I had lost when Carrie knocked into me. We worked through the steps, counting carefully as we leaped and spun. It was beginning to feel good — but I knew we had a long way to go before it would *look* good.

But then, once again, on the final *arabesque*, Carrie knocked into me — hard. This time she didn't quite fall, but our collision definitely drew Mme Noelle's attention. She frowned at me.

"But I didn't — " I began, and then I just stopped. I sounded like a baby, back in the beginner's ballet class. That kind of excuse didn't belong here. If Carrie — and Mme Noelle — wanted to blame me for what was happening, there was no point in trying to turn that blame around. It would only make me look worse.

This time, instead of speaking out, I put all my energy into the steps we were learning. I became more and more focused on what we were doing and just tried to steer clear of Carrie Steinfeld. It wasn't easy at first, but after awhile I forgot about everything except how it felt to dance.

There were no other major catastrophes for the rest of the rehearsal. And when it ended, Mme Noelle nodded at me approvingly. I think she must have sensed how hard I was working.

After rehearsal, I collapsed onto the bench in the dressing room as I pulled out my dance bag. I felt tired, but in a good way — and I felt satisfied with my dancing that day. I took my hair out of its ponytail and shook it out. Then I reached into my dance bag and I knew right away that something was wrong.

My jeans and my shirt were still in there, and so were my sneakers. But my whole spare outfit was gone. No black leotard, no pink tights. No leg warmers (I'd worn the white ones, so it was the purple ones that were missing) and no sweat shirt. No spare toe shoes, either.

"Oh, my lord," I said, under my breath. (That's one of Claudia's favorite expressions, and we've all picked it up.) I looked around to see if anyone was noticing *me* noticing my empty bag. They were all busy with their own stuff.

I shrugged. What was I going to do about it? There was a thief in our midst (as they would say in a Nancy Drew book) but I wasn't going to catch her that night. I was too exhausted even to think about it.

I pulled on my school clothes and bent over to tie my shoes. Then I saw it. Once again, a note was tucked into the laces of my left sneaker. Only this time, the note was written in blood!

I gasped. Oh, how creepy. Hiding my toe shoes was no big deal. Stealing my extra dance clothes was worse, but it still wasn't a federal offense. But a note written in blood! Ew. For a minute I thought I was going to pass out.

Then I looked closer and saw that it wasn't blood at all. It was just red ink. But this time, it didn't say BEWARE. It said: WATCH YOUR STEP. As I read it, I shivered. Then I crumpled it up and stuck it into my bag. This was getting scary. Somebody was really out to get me. But why?

I left the dressing room as quickly and quietly as I could. I didn't want to draw attention to myself. My dad picked me up, and I barely spoke to him during the ride home. He didn't try to get me to talk, even though I could tell he'd noticed that something was wrong. He's pretty sensitive that way.

As we pulled into the driveway, I made a real effort to forget all about the disturbing events of the day. I just didn't want to think about the note, or what it might mean, for awhile.

Fortunately, Becca had something besides *The Sleeping Beauty* on her mind that evening. The minute I came into the house, she came flying down the stairs, waving a piece of paper in the air.

"Why didn't you *tell* me?" she yelled happily. "I can't believe you kept this a secret."

"Tell you what?" I asked. I really didn't know what she was talking about. "What secret?"

"The pet show!" she shrieked. "It's going to be great!"

I'd forgotten all about it. "Let's see the invitation," I said. Becca handed it to me, and I unfolded it.

CALLING ALL KIDS! it said, in big red letters. Each of the letters had little animals climbing all over it — puppies and kittens and monkeys and all kinds of other beasts. Claudia is *so* talented.

The reason it said "all kids" instead of "pet owners" was that we'd decided to invite all of our regular customers — whether they had pets or not. That way, a kid like Jamie Newton, who doesn't have a pet, could still come to the show and have fun.

Underneath the headline were more pictures of animals, and then the information about the pet show: where it was going to be held, and when, and what kinds of pets could be entered. ("Bring your goldfish! Bring your pony! Bring any pet you have!")

Becca was nearly beside herself. "It came in the mail today, Jessi!" she cried. "It had my name on it! I'm invited!"

I didn't want to spoil things by telling her that *everyone* was invited. "That's great, Becca," I said. "A pet show will be fun, won't it?"

She nodded. Then her smile faded.

"But we don't have a pony. We don't even have a dog! All we have is Misty." She looked worried.

"Misty's a great pet," I said. "She's friendly, and clean, and she knows her name — "

"But she's just a hamster," said Becca. "There's no way she can win a prize at a big pet show like this."

I thought about all the other pets that would probably be entered in the show. Nobody had a pony, at least as far as I knew. But there were a lot of dogs in the neighborhood —

dogs that knew how to do all kinds of tricks. There were a lot of beautiful cats, too. Would a boring little hamster be able to compete? Becca might have a point, there, I thought. But I didn't want her to worry about it.

"Winning a prize isn't everything, Becca," I said. "Just being in the show will be fun." I thought I sounded very grown-up and reasonable.

A tear ran down Becca's cheek. "I wish we had a dog," she said. "Then I could give it a bath, and put a ribbon around its neck, and teach it some really great tricks. Then it would win first prize!" She sniffed. Obviously, she wasn't convinced by my reasonable little speech. "Dumb old Misty is just going to sit there, wiggling her nose."

"C'mon, Becca," I said. "You love 'dumb old Misty.' Remember when we got her, how excited you were?"

Misty was born during one of my craziest sitting jobs. I'd been pet-sitting for this couple, the Mancusis. They don't have any kids, but boy, do they have a lot of pets. They have three dogs, five cats, some birds, two guinea pigs, lots of fish, a snake (ew!) named Barney, a bunch of rabbits, and an aquarium full of turtles.

The Mancusis also have hamsters, and when I was sitting, one of the hamsters got sick. It was awful! I didn't know what was wrong with him, and I had to miss an important meeting of the club to take him to the vet.

Well, you've probably guessed the rest of the story. "He" was really a "she" — and she was pregnant. She was going to give birth very, very soon. And not long after the babies were born (there were a lot of them!), the Mancusis came home. They were very happy with the way I'd handled the whole thing, and they offered me a baby hamster of my own.

Of course, we didn't take Misty home until she was old enough to leave her mother. The Pikes got a hamster, too, and so did one of the kids we sit for, Jackie Rodowsky. Becca was thrilled to pieces when we got Misty — but now the thrill seemed to be wearing off. There was nothing I could say to convince her that winning a prize didn't matter. Maybe this pet show wasn't such a hot idea after all.

CHAPTER 6

Saturday

Total pet-mania. I can't believe how excited the kids are about the pet show. And guys? I hate to admit this (I really, _really_ hate to admit this), but maybe, just maybe, this pet show was not the best idea in the world. I mean, it seems to be getting just a little out of hand already — and there's still a lot of time before the show.

Kristy must have been feeling really overwhelmed. For her to admit that one of her ideas might not have been totally and completely perfect — well, let's just say that I've never heard her come close to admitting anything like that before.

That Saturday afternoon, Kristy was sitting for her brother David Michael; her adopted sister, Emily Michelle; and her stepsister and stepbrother, Karen and Andrew. Kristy had her hands full.

It was a beautiful, sunny day, and they were all sitting on the back-porch steps. Well, actually, they weren't just "sitting." David Michael was hanging over the railing, making burping noises, while Karen shrieked at him to stop. Emily was zooming her Tonka truck around Kristy's feet, screaming with glee every time she made a sharp turn. And Andrew was off in his own little world, examining an ant that he'd found crawling on the porch.

In between burps and shrieks and screams, they were all talking about — guess what — the pet show. All except Emily Michelle, that is. She doesn't talk much yet.

"I wonder who will get second prize," David Michael said. "Maybe one of the cats."

"What do you mean, second prize?" asked Karen. "What about *first* prize?"

"Well, I don't need to wonder about that," David Michael answered. "I know which pet will get first prize. Shannon will. And I'm going to enter her, so I'll get to keep the blue ribbon." He paused to think for a moment. "I wonder where I should hang it in my room," he said.

"What makes you so sure that Shannon will win?" asked Kristy.

"Well, she's the biggest pet that'll be in the show," said David Michael. (Shannon *is* pretty big — she's a Bernese mountain dog, and she'll be the size of a Saint Bernard when she's fully grown.) "And she's got the best personality, right?"

Kristy had to admit that Shannon was pretty sweet — not to mention clever and loyal.

"And she's the best-looking!" finished David Michael triumphantly. "Mega-Dog!"

Kristy raised her eyebrows. "Well, we'll see," she said vaguely. She was thinking that it might not look too good if a dog from her own family won first prize in a pet show that had been her idea to begin with.

"I don't think Shannon's so great," Andrew said. He'd gotten bored with the ant and had started to listen to David Michael's boasting. "Midgie's cuter and smarter than her any day. Midgie's gonna win. I just know it."

Midgie is this little mutt (he is cute and

smart, but he is definitely a mutt) that belongs to Andrew's stepfather, Seth.

"Did Seth say you could enter Midgie?" asked Kristy.

"Yup!" said Andrew proudly. "And I'm gonna give him a bath, and put ribbons in his hair. He's gonna look great!"

"If you put ribbons in his hair, he's going to look like even more of a wimp than he already is!" said Karen.

"Wimp?" asked Andrew.

"Yeah," said Karen. "Midgie's a wimp. He's afraid of his own shadow. He'll never win a prize — not unless you train him to do some tricks or something. And you don't have time for that."

Andrew looked downcast, but Kristy put her hand on his shoulder and gave him a squeeze. "Don't worry, Andrew," she said. "Midgie's a fun little dog, and you'll have a good time entering him in the pet show. And that's all that matters, right? Having a good time?"

(Does that sound familiar? Kristy and I had come up with the same reasonable, grown-up-sounding line. I only wished that some of the kids would start to agree with it.)

"Well, I'm going to have a good time," said Karen.

"Great!" said Kristy.

"Because *my* pet is definitely going to win first prize," Karen finished.

Kristy rolled her eyes. "What pet are you entering?" she asked.

"Well, that's the only problem," said Karen. "I can't decide between Rocky and Emily Junior."

Rocky is Seth's cat. And Emily Junior is (ew) a rat! Emily Junior lives with Karen's mother and stepfather, instead of at Watson's house.

"Rocky's kind of funny-looking," mused Karen. "I'd probably have to dress her up or something."

Kristy pictured Rocky in Karen's dress-up clothes — her "lovely lady" clothes, as she calls them. High heels, a big hat . . . or maybe a wedding veil. Kristy tried not to laugh out loud.

"But if I entered Emily Junior, she'd probably be the only rat there. Maybe she'd win a prize just for that," Karen continued. "The only thing is that I'd probably have to give her a bath, and I don't know how much she'd like that," she added. "I just can't decide."

"What about Boo-Boo?" asked David Michael. "Doesn't anybody want to enter Boo-Boo?"

Everybody laughed. Why? Because Boo-Boo is not just any cat. Boo-Boo is the oldest, fattest, and *meanest* cat you've ever seen.

"He's too nasty," said Karen. "He'd probably hiss at the judges."

"Yeah," said Andrew. "And how could we even pick him up to carry him to the show? He's too fat."

Obviously, Boo-Boo was out of the question as a pet-show contestant.

"But what about Emily Michelle?" asked David Michael. "She doesn't have a pet to enter."

"Pet!" said Emily Michelle, smiling and clapping her hands.

David Michael started to laugh all of a sudden.

"What's so funny?" asked Karen.

"What if *Emily* enters Boo-Boo?" he said.

Kristy thought of Emily trying to lug Boo-Boo to the pet show. "That cat is almost bigger than *she* is!" she said, laughing.

Karen and Andrew cracked up, too. Then Karen got serious. "But Emily's too young to enter a pet, right?" she asked Kristy.

"I think so," said Kristy. "She doesn't really understand what we're talking about." It was true. Emily Michelle was playing happily with her Tonka truck, totally absorbed in shifting a little pile of pebbles from one area to another.

"Rrrr . . ." said Emily, making a pretty good truck noise.

As the afternoon wore on, some of the other kids in Kristy's neighborhood came over to play. Hannie and Linny Papadakis were the first to arrive. They'd brought their little sister, Sari, to play with Emily. They're just about the same age, even though Sari's more advanced in some ways than Emily. Emily is having a hard time learning certain games — maybe because she had a very hard time for the first year or so of her life in Vietnam.

Hannie (she's seven, and in the same class at school as Karen) and Linny (he's eight, and he's David Michael's best friend) were just as excited about the pet show as everybody else. It was all they could talk about.

It was the same with Scott and Timmy Hsu, who live down the street, and Max and Amanda Delaney. They all gathered on Kristy's front lawn, and nobody wanted to talk about anything but the pet show.

Karen and Amanda are friends, even though Amanda can be kind of stuck-up. (Which is why Hannie can't stand her.) Max, who's six, is always trying to be friends with the other kids, but it seems that David Michael and Linny would rather avoid him.

Scott and Timmy Hsu are good kids, and everybody likes them. In fact, Hannie and Scott are married! (Well, they're pretend married. Karen just got married, too, to a boy in her class.)

Anyway, with all these kids, some of whom like each other and some of whom might be looking for a fight, Kristy thought it would be a good idea to forget the pet show for awhile and organize a game.

"How about freeze tag?" she yelled over the commotion.

"Yeah!" cried David Michael. "I'm It!" Everybody scattered, and David Michael started trying to tag them. Emily was the only one who didn't quite "get" the rules of the game. Whenever David Michael tagged her, she collapsed in a heap on the ground, giggling and shrieking as if he were tickling her to death.

"She won't stop wiggling!" complained David Michael to Kristy. "She's supposed to freeze."

Kristy told David Michael that Emily was just too young. "C'mon, Emily-bird," she said, scooping her up. "You and I will watch from the porch."

The game went on for some time, until the older kids, at least, had had a chance to be It. Then everybody flopped down on the grass, panting. Kristy brought out paper cups and a pitcher of lemonade and passed out some to all the kids.

Then they began talking about the pet show again. Karen was the one who brought it up. "Which one of you is going to enter Priscilla?" she asked Amanda and Max. (Priscilla is the Delaneys' cat.) Karen's always got her nose in everyone's business. She's kind of like a young Kristy. She's full of energy and good ideas, and sometimes she gets herself into trouble by saying things before she's really thought them out.

Like this time.

For a moment, neither Max nor Amanda answered her question. Then they both spoke up at once.

"Me!" said Max.

"I am!" said Amanda.

"She's *my* cat!" they both said, in perfect unison.

"Uh-oh," said Kristy to herself. "Trouble."

"Priscilla will be the most beautiful cat in the show," said Amanda. "Nobody else around here owns a purebred white Persian that cost four hundred dollars." Amanda has a habit of pointing out how much everything costs. I guess she *is* kind of stuck-up some-times — but she's basically a good kid. "And I intend to get first prize with her," she finished.

Before Max could argue with his sister, Han-nie jumped into the battle. "What do you mean, Priscilla is the most beautiful cat around? Pat the cat is prettier than that old dust mop any day! And smarter, too."

Pat the cat is Hannie's kitten. All the Papadakises' pets have funny rhyming names. There's Pat the cat, Noodle the poodle, and Myrtle the turtle.

"Dust mop!" repeated Amanda, outraged. "How dare you — "

"And she's a dumb dust mop, too," said Hannie. "She can't even do any tricks."

"So what?" asked Amanda. "She's a cat, not a dog. Cats aren't supposed to do tricks."

"Pat the cat can do tricks," said Hannie. "She can dance around on her hind legs." She smiled meanly at Amanda. "The judges are going to love her," she said.

Kristy thought it was time to change the subject — or at least to get the focus of the conversation off cats.

"Who are you going to enter, Linny?" she asked.

He smiled at her. Linny can be a little shy, but he's great if you draw him out. "I'm going to enter Myrtle," he said. "I'm going to paint her shell so she looks really cool."

"Great!" said Kristy. Then she looked over at Scott and Timmy. They looked a little downcast. "What about you guys?" she asked.

"We don't have any pets," said Timmy.

"So I guess we can't enter the show."

Before Kristy could begin to comfort them, Karen spoke up. "You can borrow Boo-Boo!" she said. "He might not win, but at least you'd have a pet to enter." Timmy's eyes lit up.

"And you can borrow Noodle, Scott!" said Hannie. "After all, you are my husband. Noodle's kind of like your pet, too, right?"

Kristy looked seriously at Hannie and Karen. "Are you guys sure about that?" she asked. "Lending your pet to somebody is kind of a big deal." She didn't want to see any more fights spring up.

"Hmmm . . ." said Karen. "Maybe you're right. Forget it, Timmy. What if Boo-Boo did win a prize? Then I'd be mad."

"I didn't think of that," said Hannie. "I take it back, Scott. You can't have Noodle after all."

Scott looked stunned. "I thought you said that he was my pet, too!" he said. "Does this mean we're getting a divorce?"

"I don't know," said Hannie. "Maybe. But anyway, you have to find your own pet."

Kristy groaned. It looked like the honeymoon was over for those two. And it looked like her latest idea might end up being more trouble than it was worth. The pet show was supposed to be fun — but the kids seemed to be taking it a little too seriously.

"**H**ey, Princess," said Lisa. "How's it going?"

I smiled. "Fine," I said. "I'm really up for today, aren't you?"

Lisa nodded.

"You'd better be up," said Hilary, overhearing me. "You haven't been doing too well so far. Sleeping Beauty's sleeping on the job."

I ignored her. I knew that none of the things that had happened at the first and second rehearsal had been my fault. But today would be different. Today, things would go smoothly.

It was the day of the third rehearsal, and it was time to change out of my school clothes. I pulled on my new pink tights and my new black leotard. Over the tights I pulled on my new (blue) leg warmers. I put on my new baggy sweat shirt.

"Woo, new outfit!" said Lisa. "Nice!"

"Thanks!" I said.

How did I get all that brand-new stuff? I used my hard-earned baby-sitting money, that's how. And I hated having to do it. Sure, it's nice to have new things — I retired my older things to serve as spares right away. Still, it doesn't really seem fair. I'm trying to save that money for other things. But there was no way I could get by with just one of everything — I'd learned that lesson well enough. So I bit the bullet and laid out the money.

I'd even stretched my cash to buy one other thing — something that I hoped would prevent anyone from taking my stuff ever again. It was a new dance bag. The old one had been big enough, and it was still in pretty good shape. But the new one has something that the old one didn't have. The new one has a zipper at either end, and the zipper tabs meet in the middle. Guess what. There's this tiny padlock that I can use to lock the zippers together.

Can you believe I actually have to lock up a grimy old leotard and a ratty pair of leg warmers? As my parents would say, "What *is* the world coming to?"

By the time I'd finished putting up my hair, everybody else was in the studio. Good. For some reason, I didn't want them to see me locking up my bag. I closed the bag, took out the tiny key, and made sure the little padlock was locked tight. Then I put the key on the thin gold chain I was wearing around my neck.

Mme Noelle doesn't really approve of wearing jewelry in class, so I usually don't. But she says it's okay as long as it doesn't get in the way. I tucked the necklace under my leotard and checked in the mirror. It hardly showed, so Madame probably wouldn't even notice it.

Once rehearsal started, I forgot about the key. For a change, nothing bad was happening to me, and I was free to concentrate on practicing my steps. Mme Noelle was giving me approving looks.

"Beautiful!" she said, as I *bourée*'d across the floor. "But *smile*, Mademoiselle Romsey. Relax and enjoy it!"

Oh, sure. Have you ever tiptoed across a whole floor, moving nothing but your legs in the tiniest, controlled movements? I tried to smile, but my feet were killing me. A ballet dancer's feet are almost *always* killing her.

We switched to another step, and I had a chance to relax for a moment as I waited my turn to show Mme Noelle my technique. Lisa Jones did a lovely *arabesque* at the back of the room. She was just practicing while she waited her turn. Carrie was on the floor, showing Mme Noelle her stuff.

After I took my turn, I stood again in the

little knot of dancers, waiting for Madame to tell us what was next. I heard Hilary whispering behind me, and turned quickly to warn her to be quiet. (Madame *hates* it when we whisper.) Just as I turned, I heard a tiny *clink*. I looked down. Uh-oh. My necklace had dropped to the ground. The catch must have come unfastened.

I knelt quickly and grabbed it before anyone saw. Then, still kneeling, I scrambled to fasten it around my neck. When I stood up, I realized that I had missed Mme Noelle's directions. I had no idea what we were supposed to do next — and I was out in front of the group, which meant I might have to go first.

I looked around desperately. Mme Noelle's back was turned — she was just about to put the needle down onto the record. Carrie was standing next to me.

"Quick!" I said. "What did she say?"

"*Tour jetés*," replied Carrie. "One of us at a time, across the room."

I tried to catch my breath. *Tour jetés*. No problem.

"Lead off, Mademoiselle Romsey!" said Mme Noelle.

Oh, boy. I gathered myself together and took a deep breath. Then I took off, running diagonally across the room and executing a perfect *tour jeté*. (Which is a big, running leap, in case you forgot.) Well, almost perfect. The only problem with it was the landing.

I landed like a sack of potatoes, sprawled out all over the floor. For just a second, I had no idea where I was. I shook my head and blinked. How could I have fallen so hard? Then I felt a sharp pain. My ankle was killing me. Everybody rushed over to where I was lying.

"Jessi, are you okay?" asked Katie Beth. "What happened?"

I sat up, rubbing my ankle. "I don't know. It seemed like I slipped on something when I landed." I looked around me, checking the floor. "Look!" I said, pointing to a nearby spot. "It's all wet."

Hilary knelt to look at it. "Boy, that's slick," she said. "No wonder you fell."

"Where'd that mess come from, anyway?" asked another girl.

Then Mme Noelle worked her way into the circle of girls standing around me. "You are all right, Mademoiselle Romsey?" she asked. I nodded. "Good," she said. "All of you, back to your places," she added, waving the girls away from me. She helped me up, and then she examined the wet spot on the floor.

She clapped her hands. "Lisa Jones!" she

said. "Please to run and fetch zee man who cleans zee floors!" Lisa ran out the door and headed for the janitor's room.

Madame turned back to me. I was standing there with all my weight on my right leg. My left one didn't seem to want to hold me up. "How does zee onkle feel?" she asked me, looking intently into my eyes.

I couldn't lie. "It — it hurts," I said. All I wanted to do was to keep on dancing. I could hardly stand the fact that I'd interrupted rehearsal for the third time in a row. But my ankle did hurt. A lot.

"Come," said Mme Noelle. She walked with me over to the side of the room (or rather, she walked; I limped), sat me down on a chair, and knelt in front of me. "Let's take a look," she said.

She picked up my foot and examined my ankle. Mme Noelle has seen a lot of injuries in her years of dancing — ballerinas are always hurting themselves. So she knew what she was doing. Anyway, even I could see that my ankle was swelling up and beginning to look bruised.

"Not so bad," said Mme Noelle. "It is not sprained, I sink. Just a strain. But you must see zee doctor." She looked into my face. "Tell me," she said. "Why were you performing zee *tour jeté*?"

"What do you mean?" I asked. "That's what we were supposed to be doing, wasn't it?"

She shook her head. "You were not listening well, mademoiselle. I said nossing about zee *tour jeté*. You were all to show me your best *glissade changée*."

I felt like such a fool. I must have misunderstood Carrie. "I'm so sorry, Madame Noelle," I said. "You're right. I wasn't listening well." I hung my head, ashamed. I just hate to disappoint her.

"It is all right, Jessica," said Mme Noelle gently. "Zee important sing for now is for your onkle to have zee chonce to heal." She smiled at me.

Then she dropped the bomb. "You must not donce for several days."

Not dance! But what about the production? How were they going to rehearse *The Sleeping Beauty* without me?

Mme Noelle answered my question before I even had a chance to ask it. She stood up and faced the class. "Mademoiselle Parsons," she said in a louder voice, gesturing to Katie Beth. "You will take over zee role of Princess Aurora — "

I couldn't believe my ears. Had I lost the lead role just because I'd slipped on some stupid wet spot?

" — for zee next rehearsal, and perhops

some others, until Jessica is able to donce again," she finished.

Phew. I was relieved. At least I hadn't completely lost my chance to perform as Princess Aurora. But still, I felt like crying. There haven't been too many times in my life when I've been unable to dance — but there's nothing that can make me quite as miserable. Mme Noelle says that injuries are a part of a "doncer's" life, and that we'd better get used to them. I don't know if I'll *ever* be able to take things like this gracefully.

Mme Noelle clapped her hands. "Shall we continue?" she said. Then she turned back to me. "I would like to allow you to stay and watch zee rehearsal, but I sink you need to get off zat foot. Perhops you should have your father take you to zee doctor, and then you can go home and lie down."

I nodded miserably and limped out of the studio. I couldn't help noticing, as I crossed the floor, that Katie Beth was absolutely beaming. I'm not saying that she was happy to see me get hurt — but she sure didn't look all that broken up about it.

I smiled broadly at her. I wasn't about to give her the satisfaction of seeing me miserable.

I headed for the pay phone and called my father's office. "Mr. Ramsey, please," I said when somebody answered. Then my dad picked up his extension. Just hearing his voice say "Hello?" made all the tears I'd been holding inside well up and overflow.

"Daddy!" I wailed, feeling like a two-year-old.

"Jessi!" he said. "What is it? Are you all right?" He sounded frantic.

I hadn't meant to scare him. I took a deep breath and started over. "I'm okay," I said, sniffling a little. "It's just that I hurt my ankle during rehearsal. Madame Noelle says I should see a doctor." I drew a ragged breath. "Oh, Daddy, she says I can't dance for awhile!"

"It'll be okay, sweetie," he said. "Now you sit tight. I'm on my way."

I hung up the phone and went into the dressing room to change. This had been the worst of three bad rehearsals, and in a way I was just grateful that it was over.

I looked up at the framed picture of Mikhail Baryshnikov that hangs above one of the sinks. He looked back at me, smiling his cocky smile. "Oh, Misha," I said. (I feel like I know him — he's my favorite dancer of all time — so it seems okay to use his nickname.) "I just want to crawl under a rock."

He kept on smiling, and I could swear I heard him say, "Oh, Jessi, lighten up. So you can't dance for a few days. If that's the worst that happens, that's not so bad."

I knew Misha was right. And if my mother were there she'd agree with him. "Get over it, Jessi!" she'd say. I decided to take their advice — even if it *was* all in my mind.

It was time to put all of this bad luck behind me. So I had to take a break from dancing. Big deal. When I came back, I'd be rested and better than ever.

I pulled my new dance bag out from under the bench, and my heart sank. A piece of paper was jammed over the padlock. Another note. I picked it up carefully and unfolded it. I read it and gasped. Here's what it said: I TOLD YOU SO. FROM NOW ON, WATCH OUT.

I felt a chill run down my spine. I thought of the wet spot on the floor, and how I'd slipped and fallen. Had somebody *planned* my fall? And if so, who? And why? How could anybody do such a mean thing? My head was full of questions. And my ankle was throbbing. I changed and got out of that place as quickly as I could.

CHAPTER 8

"I'm sorry, Jessi, but I have to agree with your teacher," said Dr. Dellenkamp. My dad had driven me straight to her office. She held my ankle gently as she examined it. "This looks like a pretty bad strain. Still, it could have been worse."

I nodded glumly. "I know. I could have sprained it, or even broken it, right?"

"According to what you told me, I'd have to say that you got off easy," she agreed. "But it's important that you give even a minor injury like this plenty of time to heal."

"How long do I have to stay off my foot?" I asked. I held my breath as I waited for her answer. Was that one fall — which happened so quickly — going to ruin my chance to dance the part of Princess Aurora?

"Just about three days, I'd say," she answered. "Longer if it's still sore by then."

Three days. That wasn't so bad. I ran over

the rehearsal schedule in my mind. I would only have to miss one rehearsal. I gave a sigh of relief.

"Now let's wrap it well," said Dr. Dellenkamp, pulling an Ace bandage out of a drawer. "And I'm going to give you some crutches to use, too. You really need to keep your weight off that ankle." She smiled at me. "Sound okay?"

I nodded. "Whatever you say. I just want to be dancing again as soon as possible."

My ankle hurt pretty badly that night, especially when I was trying to get to sleep. It throbbed painfully and kept me awake. Maybe it was lucky that I didn't have to dance at rehearsal the next day — I was wiped out.

It felt funny to sit on a chair against the wall in the studio and watch everybody else rehearse. Katie Beth was in her glory, dancing my part. Carrie kept shooting glances my way — and maybe it was all in my mind, but she looked kind of guilty to me. I started to wonder . . . had one of them been writing those notes? Was it only a coincidence that water had spilled on the floor? And had I really misunderstood Carrie — or did she tell me to do the wrong step on purpose?

I didn't like being so suspicious — but I was really beginning to feel scared. It seemed that somebody was out to get me — and the stakes were pretty high. Somebody wanted me out of the way so that she could dance the lead role — that seemed obvious. And she didn't care if I got hurt in the process.

After rehearsal, some of the girls gathered around the chair where I sat.

"How are you feeling, Jessi?" That was Hilary, sounding syrupy sweet. She'd never cared about my welfare before. . . .

"I'm okay," I said. "It doesn't hurt too badly. I think I'll be able to dance again by the next rehearsal."

"That's great!" said Lisa.

I looked at her closely. Was she really being sincere? Suddenly, it seemed like any one of the girls in my class could be suspected of trying to get rid of me. What a terrible feeling!

I waited until everybody else had cleared out. Then I hopped into the dressing room on my crutches. It was embarrassing to limp around like some cripple — I didn't want anyone laughing at me. I checked my locker, just to make sure there wasn't a moldy old leotard in there that I should take home and put in the wash.

There wasn't. But there *was* another note. "What's going on here?" I said out loud, as I unfolded it. Once again I saw that blood-red ink. IT COULD HAVE BEEN WORSE, it said, echoing Dr. Dellenkamp's words. But then it went on. TOO BAD IT WASN'T.

At the next BSC meeting, I poured out the story to my friends. I hadn't talked about it too much yet — mainly because I was embarrassed. It had seemed silly. Until now.

"This person, whoever she is, sounds really mean, Jessi," said Mary Anne. "This is serious."

"I know," I said. "I'm starting to get scared. What if I *really* got hurt?"

"That's what worries me," said Mallory. "But what are you going to do? Maybe you should talk to Madame Noelle."

"I can't do that," I said. "She'd never believe that such things were going on in her school. She'd think I was making it all up." I paused for a moment, while Kristy answered the phone. Should I tell them what I'd been thinking of doing?

"Actually," I said, when the job at the Papadakises' had been arranged, "I've been thinking that maybe I should just quit the production. I love that role, but it's not worth risking my life for it."

Mallory gasped. "Give up the production!" she said. "You're nuts, Jessi. That may be the best part you've ever gotten. You can't let them scare you out of it."

"Mal's right," said Claud. "You can't quit. I've already bought a new outfit to wear to your opening night." She laughed. "I'm only kidding. But really, we'll help you figure out what to do," she added.

Dawn leaned forward. "Hey, Jessi, do you still have the notes you got?"

I nodded. "They're right here," I said, digging into my new high-security dance bag.

"Let's see them," she said. I handed them over, and she started to examine each one closely. "Boy, I can see why you're feeling scared," she said, after she'd read each one. She passed them around to the others. There was a pause while everybody read them — and while Stacey answered a couple of job calls.

"Still, Jessi," said Kristy after a few minutes. "The *idea* was to scare you. You can't give this person the satisfaction."

"I've got an idea," said Mallory suddenly. "What if we came to watch one of your rehearsals? We could be — what d'you call it? Objective observers? And maybe we could finger the suspect."

I thought about it for a minute. "Our next rehearsal is on the stage where the performance is going to be held," I said slowly, fig-uring it out. "If you sat in the back of the theater, maybe no one would notice you."

"It sounds like fun," said Stacey. "But that's in Stamford, too, right? How are we going to get there?"

"No problem," said Kristy. "I bet Charlie would drive us."

Just then the phone rang, and Kristy jumped to answer it. By the time the job had been assigned, I had decided that the plan sounded good. I agreed not to drop out of the produc-tion, at least not until my friends could observe a rehearsal.

"Now that that's settled," said Kristy, "what about the pet show? I know I sounded kind of down on it in my notebook entry, but don't you all still think it'll be fun?"

She sounded like she needed to be con-vinced.

"I do!" said Mary Anne. "And I know the kids do, even if it is stirring up some com-petition. They're having fun already."

"I know," said Mallory. "I baby-sat for the Perkins girls yesterday afternoon, and you should have seen them trying to give Chewy a bath. What a mess!"

Chewy is Chewbacca, the Perkinses' dog. He's a black Labrador retriever, and boy, is he a nut. He's the most energetic dog I've ever seen — and since he's also big and strong, sometimes he creates total chaos in that house.

"First of all," said Mallory, "every time they finally wrestled him into the tub, he'd jump out again and shake water off all over the bathroom."

"Oh, no!" said Dawn, groaning. "I hope Mrs. Perkins was prepared for this."

"She said that whatever the girls wanted to do was okay," said Mallory. "I guess she figures that it's only water. Anyway, then they'd get him into the tub, and one of them would have to get in *with* him to try to hold him. The other one would pick up the bar of soap and start scrubbing. Then the soap would slip out of her hands and onto the floor, and Chewy — "

"Would jump out to retrieve it, I bet!" finished Dawn. "That dog can never let anything drop to the ground without running to pick it up."

"No joke!" said Mallory. "He looked pretty surprised the first time he picked up the soap. It must have tasted so gross! But he kept doing it again and again."

"So did he finally get clean?" asked Stacey.

"He was getting there," said Mallory. "But then Gabbie left the room for a minute and came back carrying R.C."

That's R.C. for Rat Catcher, the Perkinses' brown tiger cat.

"She must have thought R.C. needed a bath, too — because the next thing I knew, she'd dumped her in the tub with Chewy!"

Oh, my lord.

"R.C. jumped right out and streaked out the door, looking like a drowned rat. And Chewy chased after her. Water was flying all over the place!" said Mallory. By now we were hysterical, imagining the scene.

"Of course, R.C. ran under the porch, and Chewy followed her. Both of them got covered with dirt. So the whole thing was a waste!"

"I'm sure Chewy would have gotten dirty again by the time of the pet show, anyway," said Mary Anne.

"That's what I tried to tell Gabbie and Myriah," said Mallory. "But they were too upset to listen. What a day! It took us the rest of the afternoon to clean up the bathroom."

"I had kind of a similar experience with Linny Papadakis and his turtle," said Kristy.

"He gave his *turtle* a bath?" asked Claudia.

"No, he didn't exactly give Myrtle a bath," said Kristy. "What happened was — " But she was interrupted by a job call. Mrs. Barrett needed a sitter for Buddy, Suzi, and Marnie. Mallory got the job. Then Kristy went on with her story.

"Linny spent all afternoon painting Myrtle's shell," she said. "He used these water-based poster paints, since I told him that his model paints might not be so good for Myrtle. You know what? He did a great job. Myrtle looked really cool when he was done."

"What did he paint?" asked Claudia.

"There were these red lightning bolts running down the sides of the shell, and yellow stars," said Kristy. "And all kinds of other stuff. We took Myrtle outside with us afterward, so that Linny could admire her once in awhile as he played."

"Sounds like a disaster is coming up!" said Mary Anne.

"You're right," said Kristy. "Linny got involved in a game of Statues with some other kids, and Myrtle crawled over to this little plastic pool in the side yard. By the time we got to her, all the paint had washed off."

"Oh, poor Linny!" I said.

"I know," said Kristy. "He was really crushed. But at least he learned that he's got to keep Myrtle away from water if he wants the paint job to last."

We talked about the pet show for the rest of our meeting that day — it was clearly the "main event" for a lot of kids in Stoneybrook. I only hoped we'd all live through it.

CHAPTER 9

Thursday

Why, oh why did we ever think that a pet show would be fun? So far it seems to be causing nothing but messes, and tears, and trouble of every kind. I should have known that the pet show had something to do with the way Buddy and Suzi were acting... Oh, well, I guess it worked out in the end. And so will the pet show. Right, guys? Right?

Poor Mallory. She realized the minute she entered the Barretts' house that she was in for a bad afternoon. As usual, Mrs. Barrett was running late (she's sort of disorganized), and she left without giving Mallory any instructions about the job. (We always get to jobs on time — or even early — so that parents can let us know if they have any special directions for us. But in Mrs. Barrett's case, arriving early hardly ever does any good.)

Mrs. Barrett was divorced not too long ago, and I guess caring for three kids on her own isn't easy. I'll say one thing, though — it doesn't take a toll on her appearance. Mrs. Barrett is totally gorgeous. She looks like a model, with her beautiful chestnut-colored hair. Anyway, Mrs. Barrett rushed out as Mallory came in, leaving a cloud of perfumed air behind her.

She also left three cranky kids. Buddy, who's eight, is usually in a pretty good mood — and he's always got a lot of energy. But that afternoon he seemed sulky and withdrawn. And five-year-old Suzi's round face looked crabby. She can pout with the best of them. Mallory said that Suzi's lower lip was stuck out about as far as it could go.

Marnie, the baby (she's two), was wailing like a fire engine. Mallory scooped her up.

"What is it, Marnie?" she asked. But the answer was obvious. Marnie's diaper was soaking wet.

"C'mon, you guys," said Mallory to Buddy and Suzi. "Keep me company while I change your sister. Then we'll have a snack, okay?"

Buddy shot Suzi a Look. "Do I have to?" he asked. "I don't even want to be in the same room with her." He pointed at Suzi, who pouted even harder.

"Guess what, Buddy Barrett," said Suzi.

"What?" said Buddy, flatly.

"You're a nut!" Ordinarily, this joke gets a big laugh out of both of them. But this time, Buddy just shook his head.

"Guess what," he said back to Suzi.

"What?" she asked.

"Your whole family's a nut," Buddy sneered.

"Ha, ha!" said Suzi triumphantly. "You're *in* my family. That means you're a nut, just like I said."

Mallory could see that this was going nowhere. "Okay, okay," she said. "C'mon, let's get this diaper changing over with. Suzi, where has your mom been keeping the diapers lately?" The Barretts' house is pretty messy. "A pigsty," Stacey called it, the first time she sat there.

Sometimes we try to tidy up while we're

there, but Mallory didn't think that was a good idea, with Buddy and Suzi in such bad moods. So she asked Suzi to lead her to the diapers (Suzi and Marnie share a room), and asked Buddy to help her distract Marnie while she changed the wet diaper.

"Moonie, Meanie, Mownie!" said Buddy, dancing around the changing table and making faces while Mallory wiped Marnie's bottom. His technique wasn't the greatest, but Mal had to admit that it worked. Marnie was smiling and waving at him, instead of crying and kicking. She's usually not too crazy about having her diaper changed, so the distraction helped a lot.

"Thanks, Buddy," said Mallory. "Thanks, Suzi. You guys were a big help." She lifted up the newly dry Marnie, who was making what Buddy and Suzi call her "ham face," which she only does when she's happy. Then she led them back downstairs. "Now let's have a snack and you can tell me why you're both feeling so cranky today."

"I'm not cranky!" whined Suzi.

"Yes, you are, too!" said Buddy. "But I'm not. I'm *happy!*" He gave Mallory a big — and very fake — smile.

Mallory shrugged and turned to get some crackers out of the cupboard.

"Ow!" she heard, behind her. She turned

around. Suzi was rubbing her shin. "He kicked me," she said, pointing at Buddy. Mallory gave Buddy a Look.

"Buddy, don't kick your sister," she said, turning back to the cupboard.

"Hey!" This time it was Buddy's voice.

"What *is* it?" asked Mallory. She'd had just about enough of their squabbling.

"She poked me!" said Buddy.

"Did not!" yelled Suzi.

"Gobbydoo," said Marnie, waving her hands in the air.

Mallory put her hands on her hips. "Okay, that's it. I want to know what's going on between you two. You usually have a great time together. So what's the problem today?"

Suzi looked at Buddy.

Buddy glared at Suzi.

"It's Pow," they both said at once.

"I want to enter him in the pet show," said Buddy. "He's my dog. I got him for my second birthday, when he was just a puppy. Suzi wasn't even born yet then."

"But Mommy said he belongs to all of us now!" said Suzi. "And I help you feed him sometimes. *I* want to put him in the pet show!"

Pow is the Barretts' basset hound. Buddy sometimes likes to tell sitters that Pow is the meanest dog in the world. But he's not. He's

94

sleepy and slow and puts up very well with the kids' teasing.

Mallory sighed. She'd left her own house hearing a similar fight between her brothers and sisters. Ever since the Pikes had gotten their invitation to the pet show, they'd been squabbling over which one of them should be able to enter Frodo.

Frodo is the Pikes' hamster. They got him when my family got Misty, which means that he and Misty are brother and sister. I'm not great at long division, but I do know one thing: One hamster doesn't go evenly into seven kids. Mallory told me later she'd given up on helping her brothers and sisters decide which of them should enter Frodo in the show. It seemed impossible.

"I know you guys can work this out," said Mallory to Buddy and Suzi. Actually, she had her doubts about that, but she knew she had to say something. "It's really nothing to fight about. Let's finish up our snack and go outside to play." Being outside just *had* to be better than being cooped up inside with these sour-pusses, she thought.

After the kids had eaten, Mallory tidied up the kitchen (including washing a sink full of breakfast dishes that Mrs. Barrett had left behind). Then she herded her charges out the door. Marnie climbed into her stroller, and

Mallory pushed her down the front walk. Suzi ran to show Mal all the flowers that she and her mom had planted. Buddy tagged along behind them, making faces behind Suzi's back.

Then Mal saw him smile and wave. She looked up to see Haley and Matt Braddock waving back. Mallory smiled with relief. Great! Now Buddy and Suzi would have something to do besides pick on each other.

She called hello, and also made the "hello" sign to Matt. Matt's deaf, so we've all learned at least a little bit of sign language. Haley makes a great interpreter (she's fluent in sign) but it's nice to be able to "speak" to Matt directly, too.

Matt signed back. Then he and Buddy signed quickly to each other.

"What are they saying?" Mallory asked Haley.

"Matt asked if Buddy wanted to play ball, and Buddy said yes," she answered. "Hey, can me and Suzi play, too?" she asked the boys, signing as she spoke.

The game was organized within minutes, and Mal and Marnie settled in to watch.

"And it's a high pop fly to center field!" yelled Buddy, after he'd hit a blooper over Matt's (the pitcher's) head. "A triple!" He ran around the yard, pretending to tag the bases.

Then it was Haley's turn to bat. "Watch

out," she said, swinging the bat. "I'm going to hit it out of the park!" She put down the bat to sign the same thing to Matt. He signed something back, laughing.

"What do you mean, girls can't hit?" yelled Haley. She gave a mighty swing and missed completely. "Darn," she said. She shook back her hair and dug her feet into the grass. "Pitch me another one," she said, signing along. This time, she connected. Buddy (still standing on "third base") and Matt watched the ball fly over their heads. Haley forgot to run — she just stood there and watched the ball disappear.

And disappear it did — right onto the porch roof. "Great hit, Haley!" said Mallory.

"Yeah, just great!" said Buddy. "Now we've lost the ball. Why couldn't you have just hit it into the backyard?" he asked Haley. "Then Pow would have found it, no matter where it went."

"Oh, Pow Pow Pow," said Haley. "That's all I ever hear about these days is what a great dog Pow is and how he's going to win the pet show." She frowned at Buddy. "I don't think Pow is *that* great a dog," she added.

"Well, he's a lot better than no dog at all," said Buddy.

Haley bit her lip. Just then, Matt came over and looked at her questioningly. She signed to him, letting him know what Buddy had said. Matt gave Buddy a dirty look. Then he signed back to Haley.

"He says, 'So what if we don't have a pet?' " Haley explained. "We're still invited to the pet show, you know."

"But you can't win a prize," said Suzi.

"Well, what makes you so sure *you'll* win any prizes with that fat old mutt?" asked Haley.

Suzi burst into tears. "Pow is *not* a mutt," she wailed. "He's a purebred basset hound."

Mallory decided it was time to step in. "Okay, you guys. Let's not fight about it — " she began. But Buddy was shouting at Suzi, drowning Mallory out.

"You're right, he's a basset hound. But you're not going to win any ribbons with him, anyway. *I* am!"

Oh, no, thought Mallory. Not *that* fight again. She stepped toward Buddy, ready to separate him from the others before he got any angrier.

Just then, Haley shrieked. "You don't have to *pinch* me!" she said angrily to Suzi. Then she took Matt's hand and started to drag him out of the yard. "C'mon," she said, forgetting to sign as she spoke. "Let's get out of here."

Matt seemed to know what she'd said even without the signs. He gave one last angry glance back at Buddy and Suzi, and stalked out of the yard at his sister's side.

"Oh, great," said Mallory. "Look, it's time to quit this fighting." She sat Buddy and Suzi down on the porch steps. Marnie, still in her stroller, had fallen asleep — and the fight hadn't even woken her up.

"Look, you guys. There's no rule that says that only one person can enter each pet in the pet show," said Mallory. She'd been thinking the problem over, and had come to realize that this was the only solution. "Why don't you enter Pow — together!"

Buddy and Suzi looked at each other hopefully. Mal could see that they both thought it was a good idea, but neither one wanted to be the first to give in.

"You could be in charge of his looks, Suzi," said Mal, trying to push the idea. "And Buddy, you could teach him some new tricks. How about it?"

Buddy and Suzi smiled at each other. "Yeah!" said Buddy. "Maybe I can teach him how to roll over, just like Aunt Jo's dog does!"

"And I can give him a bath, and paint his toenails pink, and put ribbons on him," said Suzi. "He'll look so, so beautiful!"

They ran off to find Pow, leaving Mal alone on the porch. She shook her head and spoke to the still-sleeping Marnie. "Sweetie, that was a close one," she said. "I thought they were going to do each other in this time." Marnie shifted in the stroller and smiled in her sleep.

Later that afternoon, her job over, Mal walked back to her house. She was hoping desperately that her brothers and sisters would have settled the Frodo issue while she was away. She couldn't take any more fighting that day.

Luckily for her, they had. For some reason — nobody knew why — the triplets had suddenly given up their claim to Frodo. They'd said that Nicky could enter him in the show, and Nicky had generously agreed to share him with Vanessa, Claire, and Margo.

Mallory was too grateful for the peaceful atmosphere at home — and too tired — to wonder about the triplets' motives for very long. She knew they must be up to something. But she'd wait for the pet show to find out what they had up their sleeves.

CHAPTER 10

"Claudia, do you *mind?*"

"What, Stacey?"

"Your elbow. It's in my ear!"

"I can't help it, Stace! There's nowhere else to put it."

"Can't you move over a little?"

"Not with Mallory in my lap, I can't. Anyway, I don't think I'll ever be able to move my legs again — there's no feeling left in them."

Mallory squealed. "Stop it, Claudia! I'm not really that heavy, am I?" she asked, trying to shift her weight.

Six of us were packed into Charlie's car, the Junk Bucket (Mary Anne couldn't come; she had a sitting job), and believe me, it was a tight squeeze. It was a rainy Saturday afternoon. We were on our way to Stamford. I had a rehearsal, and everybody else was coming to watch it.

Kristy and I were in the front seat with Charlie; I got to ride up front so that I could give him directions to the civic center. Dawn, Stacey, Claudia, and Mallory were all jammed into the backseat, and they'd been complaining about how squished they were ever since we'd pulled out of Claudia's driveway. (We'd all met there to wait for Charlie and Kristy.)

"Hey, who pinched me?" asked Dawn. Then there was a whole lot of squealing and giggling from the backseat, while everybody pinched everybody else.

"Hey, chill out back there," said Charlie, looking in the rearview mirror. "How am I supposed to drive with all that racket?"

They were quiet for a moment. Then, as Charlie stopped for a red light, Dawn saw a cute guy walking across the street, holding a newspaper over his head to keep off the rain. "Woooo!" she said loudly. "Follow that guy!"

"Dawn!" said Kristy, blushing. "Stop it! What if he hears you?"

"He can't hear her," said Claudia. "The windows are rolled up. Watch — I'll prove it. Hey, gorgeous!"

The guy turned around and stared at the Junk Bucket. All of us ducked down in our seats, giggling. "Can you believe it?" asked Claud. "Do you think he heard me? Oh, I'm going to die!"

"Well, please don't die in my car," said Charlie. "What would I tell your parents? Now, come on, quiet down."

"Okay, Charlie," said Claud. "I'm sorry." For a few minutes, there was silence from the backseat. Then the giggling started up again, as Stacey and Claudia discussed Jennifer Cooke's latest outfit.

I was hoping that Charlie wouldn't get too mad and put us all out on the street to walk the rest of the way. I was nervous enough about this rehearsal, and I at least wanted to be on time for it. But Charlie kept his cool. And actually, I was glad for the distraction that the rest of my friends were providing. It kept me from thinking too much about the rehearsal.

Why was I nervous? Well, for one thing, I was worried about my dancing lately. All the little "accidents" during class and the notes were really throwing me off, and I knew I wasn't dancing as well as I usually do. I was worried that Mme Noelle would lose patience with me if I didn't shape up soon.

Also, I knew that I really shouldn't be letting my friends come to this rehearsal. I hadn't asked Madame's permission — mainly because I'd been pretty sure she'd say no — and I was worried that they'd be caught. Then we'd *all* be in trouble.

I was also a little nervous about having to

dance in front of an audience — even if they were my friends — so early into a production. Usually there was absolutely no audience until the dress rehearsal. Would having them there affect my performance? What would they think of my dancing?

I tried to shove all my worries to the back of my mind. "Hey, Mal," I said, "let's get our hair done there, sometime!" I pointed out the window to this funny little beauty shop I've always noticed on my way into Stamford. Carmelita's Casa de Beauty, it was called. There were pictures in the window of ladies with towering hairdos, their hair teased and curled into fluffy mounds.

"Great," said Mallory. "We'll look like poodles." She giggled. "Maybe we'd win first prize at the pet show!"

"The pet show," groaned Kristy. "Please, let's forget about the pet show for one day. I've heard enough about it to last a lifetime!"

Just then, Charlie pulled into the civic center's parking lot. "Okay, everybody out!" he said. "Jessi, how are they supposed to get inside?" he asked me.

"They can use that side door," I said, pointing. "Can you help everyone sneak in? It's going to be dark in the back of the theater."

By then, the BSC members had piled out of

the backseat. "Good luck, Jessi," said Mallory. "We'll be watching!"

"And taking notes," said Dawn. She held up a little notebook and a tiny flashlight shaped like a pen.

"Wow," I said. "You guys are serious about this detective stuff. Please be careful — and don't get caught."

"We won't," said Claudia. "Don't worry — just forget we're even here. Have a good rehearsal, Jessi!"

I waved at them as they headed for the side entrance, led by Charlie. I knew he'd help get them settled before he took off to do the errands he'd been planning to do for his mother and Watson.

Then I turned and went into the backstage entrance. I shivered a little as I opened the door, remembering the excitement of the other performances I'd danced in. I only hoped that *The Sleeping Beauty* would come off as well as they had.

I changed quickly in the crowded dressing room, and then headed for the stage. Mme Noelle was waiting. I peered past her, into the darkened theater. Where were my friends? I couldn't see — or hear them — anywhere. Good. If I couldn't see them, nobody else could, either.

"Are we ready to donce today?" asked Mme Noelle, looking at me curiously. She must have been wondering what I was looking for. "Ready, Madame," I answered. And I was. So far, the rehearsal looked like it was going to go smoothly. None of my clothes had disappeared, no notes had been shoved into my bag. Today I was going to concentrate on my dancing.

At first, it was hard to forget that my friends were sitting out there in the dark, watching my every move. But before long, I did forget. I got caught up in the beautiful — and difficult — movements of the ballet, and I forgot everything. My ankle was completely healed. It felt as strong as ever.

It was a great rehearsal. I danced well, and so did everyone else. We went through pretty much the whole ballet, with plenty of stops and starts and corrections from Mme Noelle.

"Watch zee shoulder, Mademoiselle Romsey," she called as I danced. "It is still dropping during your *glissade*."

I concentrated even harder, paying attention to nothing but my muscles and my form. I didn't come close to stumbling or falling, and neither did anyone else.

"Very good!" said Mme Noelle when we were finished. "All of you are doncing wiz incredible grace today. Zee performance will be a success!"

She clapped her hands and sent us to the dressing room. While I was changing into my street clothes I thought about the rehearsal. I hoped it hadn't been a total waste for my friends. After all, nothing had happened. I have to admit that I had secretly been hoping that something *would* happen — just so they could see it firsthand.

But that day's rehearsal had been completely normal. And there was nothing suspicious in the dressing room, either. No notes, no stolen belongings. Dawn sneaked into the dressing room after a bunch of people had gone. She wanted to "investigate" — but there was nothing new for me to show her. Had the mystery been in my mind all along? Maybe I was just imagining things. Maybe I was going crazy.

"No way!" said Claudia, when I said this in the car on the way home. "I'm sure there's foul play going on. And I can guess who might be responsible, too!"

"You *can*?" I asked. "How?"

"Just by watching everybody closely," she said. "And by trying to figure out what Nancy Drew would think if she were in this situation."

"She's right," said Dawn. "I know *I* saw a few things going on. For example, why did Katie Beth make a face when Mme Noelle told you that your bore-ay — whatever *that* is — was 'close to perfect'?"

Luckily, my friends had been to enough of my performances so that they could identify most of the dancers in my class.

"I guess she might have been a little jealous," I said thoughtfully. "After all, she got to dance my role while my ankle was healing, and Mme Noelle never said anything like that about her *bourrée*."

"So . . . would she get your role if you couldn't dance it?" asked Stacey. "I mean, that would explain everything, wouldn't it? She's trying to get rid of you so she can have the lead role."

I shifted in my seat until I was looking at Stacey. "I don't know . . ." I said slowly. "I don't think that's necessarily the answer. Because if I couldn't dance, Mme Noelle would probably reaudition the whole class for the part. She's always fair that way. I don't think Katie Beth would automatically get the part — and Katie Beth must know that, too."

"What about Hilary?" asked Claudia.

"What about her?" I asked.

"Why does she look so worried all the time?" asked Claudia. "It's like she's terrified that she might do something wrong."

I explained about Hilary's mother — how pushy she is, and how she always expects Hilary to be perfect. "I know she's under a lot of pressure," I said. "I kind of feel sorry for her."

"Well, don't lose sleep over it," said Claudia. "She's not too crazy about you."

"What do you mean?" I asked.

"Oh, just a feeling I got from watching her," said Claudia. "You know how they say 'If looks could kill'? Well — she was giving *you* some looks that could stop an elephant in its tracks, if you know what I mean."

I thought that over for a minute. "So who else do you guys suspect?" I asked.

"What about Lisa Jones?" asked Mallory. "She just seems so sweet and good all the time. Nobody's *that* nice."

"You know something?" I said. "She really *is* that nice. She was worried about me when I hurt my ankle. She was the only one who called me at home that night to see how I was."

"Maybe she just wanted to find out early if you were going to be dropping out," said Kristy.

"No," I said. "I'm positive she isn't a suspect. We'll have to rule her out. I like Lisa too much to be suspicious of her."

"Okay, forget Lisa," said Claudia. "What about that old Carrie Steinfeld? What's her story?"

"Well," I said, giggling, "you hit the nail on the head by calling her 'old.' Carrie's the oldest one in our class, and this is the last performance she'll be in." I told them a little about why she needed good roles on her résumé. "I know that getting the lead would have meant a lot to her," I went on. "But she did get a pretty big role. I think the Lilac Fairy will help her out. Anyway, she's a good dancer. I'm sure she won't have trouble getting into another school."

"*You* might be sure, but maybe she's not," said Claud. "Personally, I think she's a suspect."

"I agree," said Mallory. "And I think Hilary Morgan is one, too — just based on those dirty looks she was giving you."

"Hmmm . . ." I said. "Just the two of them?"

"No," said Kristy. "I've got to vote for Katie Beth, too. Remember, you guys were enemies way back when — "

"But we made up!" I said, interrupting.

"I know," said Kristy. "But I think she's still got it in for you. And she wants that role so badly she can almost taste it."

"I don't agree," said Dawn. "I mean, if she was going to get it automatically, fine. But she'll have to audition just like everybody else, and even I can tell that there are plenty of better dancers in the class."

We argued back and forth for awhile, but by the time we had reached Stoneybrook we'd narrowed it down to three suspects: Katie Beth, Carrie, and Hilary. Now all I had to do was to keep a close eye on all of them. My friends were sure it'd be a snap to catch the guilty party.

Charlie dropped me off at my house, and as I waved good-bye, I felt grateful to my friends. I also felt relieved. I wasn't positive that we were any nearer to identifying the 'phantom of the dance school,' as Claudia had begun to call her. But I felt a little more in control of the situation. At least we'd begun to work on the mystery. And I knew that with everyone's help, I could solve it eventually.

CHAPTER 11

I watched the three suspects as closely as I could during the next few rehearsals, but things went pretty smoothly. Our practice was starting to pay off. The performance was coming together, and I was feeling more and more confident as I danced the part of Princess Aurora.

I began to think that maybe the phantom really *had* been just in my mind. Then, mysterious things began to happen again.

First, I reached into my dance bag after one rehearsal, and I found my old leotard — the one that had been stolen. But there was no way I could wear it again. It had been cut to shreds. Somebody had gone after that leotard with a sharp pair of scissors. That was creepy.

Then, during another rehearsal, I got shoved — by someone I didn't see — into some scenery that was being painted. My leotard was covered with red paint, and Mme

Noelle wasn't pleased. Neither was I. I had spent all my savings to replace my dance outfit when it was stolen, so I had to borrow money from my parents to replace it again.

This role was getting expensive.

Sometimes I wondered if it was worthwhile — if I should just give up playing Princess Aurora. But then I would spend two hours working with Mme Noelle on a segment of the ballet, and I would realize that there was no way I could give up that kind of experience.

My favorite part of the ballet was the dance I had to do when I first came on stage — the Rose Adagio. Some dancers have said that it's this dance that makes the role of Princess Aurora such a challenge, because you have to do it "cold" — without warming up on some easier dancing first.

But I loved that dance. It was full of slow, graceful movements. According to the fairy tale, this dance shows the princess being presented to the court on her sixteenth birthday. She is meeting four princes. They all want to marry her, even though she's so young.

Each prince gives her a beautiful rose, and she dances with them. But after dancing, she gives the flowers to her mother. She's having too much fun to think about serious things like marriage.

The dance that she does (or rather, that I did) with the princes is very difficult. Mme Noelle worked with us for a long time before we could do it well. The way it went was this: As I finished dancing with each prince, he helped me to balance on the point of one toe — and then he took away his hand and left me balancing there until the next prince came to dance with me.

"Do not wobble, Mademoiselle Romsey!" cried Mme Noelle as I did my best to balance on one toe. "Smile!"

I tried to smile.

"Remember, you are a joyous young princess. You must show us zee excitement and hoppiness of youth!"

I tried to act "hoppy." It wasn't easy, especially with Hilary Morgan glaring at me from the sidelines. Sometimes I felt bad about how much time Mme Noelle was spending with me, but the fact was that my role was very demanding. Still, I could tell that the other girls were jealous, and I really couldn't blame them. I would have been jealous, too.

But my phantom took jealousy a little too far. When I went into the dressing room on the day I'd been working on the Rose Adagio, I saw it right away. A note — in that same red ink — with a red rose attached. WATCH OUT FOR THE THORNS, it said.

I stood looking at it for a moment. It gave me a creepy feeling in the pit of my stomach. Then I folded the note and tucked it into my bag. I looked at the rose, thinking that I'd take it home to my mom — at least it was pretty, and it probably smelled good. But when I picked it up, a thorn pricked my finger. "Ouch!" I said out loud. I squeezed my finger and a drop of blood oozed out.

I looked around the dressing room to see who was there. Sure enough, all three suspects were among the dancers who were busy changing. Hilary was at the mirror, checking her hair. Katie Beth was by her locker — she was packing her dance clothes into her bag. And Carrie was just about to leave, but when she heard my little cry of pain, she turned around.

"Are you okay, Jessi?" she asked, coming over to me. Then she saw the rose. "Hey, that's pretty. Who's sending you flowers?"

I shrugged.

"A secret admirer, huh? Hey, everybody, Jessi's got a boyfriend!" she yelled.

I was totally embarrassed. I tossed the rose into the garbage and got out of the dressing room as soon as I could, trying not to listen to the teasing that was going on. Dancing the Rose Adagio was never quite as much fun after that day. I was always thinking of that thorn pricking my finger, like a bee sting — and of that drop of red blood appearing afterward.

But unlike Princess Aurora, I didn't fall asleep for a hundred years after I pricked my finger. Instead, I became more alert. I was dying to catch the phantom in the act.

I thought of hiding in the dressing room so that I could be there when she stuck a note into my bag. But that wouldn't work. Mme Noelle would notice my absence from rehearsal right away, since I was in almost every act. All I could do was wait — and watch.

I watched very closely. I tried to pay attention to where each of the three suspects was at all times. But it wasn't easy. Mme Noelle kept me busy throughout almost every rehearsal.

One day, Carrie bumped into me about three times during rehearsal. That day, I was sure that she was the phantom.

At another rehearsal, I overheard Hilary whispering mean things about me to Lisa Jones. I was convinced that Hilary was the one who was out to get me.

Then Katie Beth started to give me funny looks. I'd catch her watching me as I put on my toe shoes, or staring at me during exercises at the *barre*. I certainly couldn't rule her out, either.

I was getting more and more confused, and

to make it worse, the notes kept coming.

GIVE UP THE ROLE BEFORE IT'S TOO LATE, said one. I shook my head and tucked it into my bag with the rest.

After the next rehearsal, there was another. YOU HAVE BEEN WARNED, it said.

But you know what? Instead of scaring me, those notes started to make me angrier and angrier. I became more determined to solve this mystery and find out who the phantom was. Then I'd tell everything to Mme Noelle, and the performance — with me as Princess Aurora — would go off without a hitch.

One day, Carrie was absent from rehearsal. She was home with the flu, according to Madame. That day we worked extra hard on one of the most difficult parts of the dance.

When we're learning a dance, Mme Noelle makes us do the movements over and over again, until it finally looks right. Even once we've learned the basic steps, we keep repeating them. If we do even one little thing wrong, she makes us do it over again. If we do it right, we *still* have to do it again — "for luck."

Rehearsals can be so exhausting.

That day, I was ready to drop as I headed into the the dressing room. The last thing I needed was to find another note. But there it was, in that creepy red ink. TAKE A REST,

SLEEPING BEAUTY! I rolled my eyes as I put the note away. When was this going to end?

Then I realized something. Carrie was absent And I'd still received a note. Finally, I was getting somewhere with this mystery. I could rule out Carrie, which would leave me with only two suspects.

Unless . . . had Carrie only been *pretending* to be sick — and gotten someone to leave the note *for* her? I shook my head. That was pretty unlikely. She wouldn't miss a rehearsal unless she really had to.

So it was down to Katie Beth and Hilary. How was I going to figure out which one of them it was? I decided just to wait and see what would happen. If I could rule one of them out, I'd have my phantom.

Carrie was still sick at the next rehearsal. I felt bad for her, missing all that practice time. Now that I knew she wasn't the phantom, I kind of missed having her around.

But it was a relief to have to watch only two suspects instead of three. I found that I could concentrate better — and it showed in my dancing. Mme Noelle told me that I was *magnifique* that day. That's "magnificent" in French.

It always feels great to have Mme Noelle compliment you. She doesn't say nice things unless she really means them. So that afternoon I was feeling terrific. I danced the Rose Adagio without missing a step. My *pas de deux* with the Bluebird of Happiness was nearly perfect. And I got through the scene where the prince kisses me without giggling once. It was a great rehearsal.

It was great, that is, until I almost got beaned by some scenery.

In that theater, most of the scenery is painted on huge flats that can be raised and lowered on ropes. When they're in the raised position, the ropes are securely tied so they can't fall. And when it's time for the scene to change, the flat is slowly let down to the floor. Each flat must weigh about a ton — they're so big!

There were a lot of different flats for the *Sleeping Beauty* scenery. There was the grand ballroom, the magic forest, and the sleeping castle, where Princess Aurora lies awaiting her prince. I'd gotten used to the flats moving up and down during rehearsals, while the stage managers practiced their cues just like we practiced ours.

Anyway, that day I had just finished my final dance with the prince, and I was walking to the rear of the stage so that I could collapse quietly while Mme Noelle went over her notes on who — and what — needed improvement.

I didn't even see the flat falling. Before I

knew what was happening, someone had pushed me out of the way. The flat hit the stage with a loud crash, right where I had been standing only seconds before.

I felt dizzy. Was this another "accident"? I looked around, trying to get my bearings. Someone was standing next to me, asking if I was all right. It was Katie Beth. She was the one who had pushed me out of the way.

"Thanks, Katie Beth!" I said, as soon as I could speak. "I hate to imagine what would have happened if that thing had hit me!"

"I'm glad it didn't," she said, smiling at me. "Are you sure you're okay?"

She was being so nice. I felt terrible for ever being suspicious of her. "I'm fine," I said. "Thanks again."

Rehearsal ended a few minutes later. I walked off the stage and into the dressing room, thinking hard. So Carrie wasn't sending me those notes, and obviously Katie Beth wasn't, either. Was Hilary really the phantom? And if she was, how could I prove it?

That's what I asked my friends later that day at a club meeting. I'd filled them in on my detective work so far, and they were excited to hear that the pool of suspects had been narrowed down to one.

"You're almost there!" said Stacey.

"But I still have to prove that Hilary is the phantom," I said. "Any ideas?"

Everybody thought for a few minutes. Finally Kristy said, "You have to set up some kind of trap for her," said Kristy. "Let her prove her own guilt."

"But how?" asked Claudia. Then a light seemed to turn on in her eyes. "Let me see those notes again, Jessi!"

I handed them to her. Luckily I'd saved every one. Dawn leaned over to examine them again with Claudia.

"You don't see writing like this every day," said Dawn. "I noticed that before, when I looked at the first few."

"You're right," said Claudia slowly. "And I know why the writing looks so different. It's because the writer is using a special pen — the kind you do calligraphy with."

"Calligraphy? What's that?" asked Mary Anne.

"It's the fancy writing on wedding invitations and stuff like that," said Claudia. "It's pretty and slanted — and some parts of the letters are thick and other parts are thin. A girl in my art class has a calligraphy pen. It has a sharp, flat point and you can write thick *or* thin, depending on how you hold the pen."

"So what are you getting at?" asked Kristy.

"Well, all Jessi has to do is to trap Hilary into writing something, so she can see if the samples match," said Claud, smiling.

"Whoa!" said Stacey. "Claud, you're the Nancy Drew of Stoneybrook."

Claudia blushed. "Oh, yeah?" she said. "Well, if I'm Nancy Drew, who's Bess?"

We all laughed. Bess is Nancy Drew's "plump" sidekick, the one who's always eating.

"How come detectives always have a chubby friend?" asked Mallory. "There's one in the Hardy Boys, too — and in the Three Investigators. Did you ever notice that?"

Claudia laughed. "I know. I guess it's all just part of being a super crime solver. So, Stace, you're just going to have to gain some weight!" She stuck an elbow into Stacey's side, and we all cracked up.

I thought Claudia's idea was great. Now all I had to do was figure out how to get Hilary to write something — in front of me.

CHAPTER 12

For the next few days, I spent most of my free time just thinking. I had to figure out a foolproof way to trap Hilary. But for the longest time I couldn't think of a single good idea.

During rehearsals, I watched Hilary out of the corner of my eye. She was no dummy, I knew that. It wasn't going to be simple to trick her into confessing. But that's what I had to do.

For awhile I considered looking through her locker, checking to see if she owned a pen like the one Claud had described. But that seemed risky — and it didn't feel right to me. Just because she *might* be the person who had stolen my stuff didn't make it all right for me to poke through her things.

Then I thought I could just ask her to write something down for me. I'd tell her that I was doing a school project — about how to analyze handwriting. No, that was too farfetched. She'd never believe me.

If only we went to the same school, I could ask her if I could borrow her notes from a certain class. But Hilary goes to a private school. So that was out. I was at a dead end.

Finally, in desperation, I called Mallory one night. I had been trying not to take up too much of the club's time with my problem, but after all, Mal was my best friend. If I couldn't ask her for help, who could I ask? I dialed her number.

Somebody answered in a tiny little voice. "Hello?"

"Hi, Claire," I said. "This is Jessi."

"Hi," she replied, breathing into the phone.

"Is Mallory there?" I asked.

"Yes," she said. But she didn't ask if I wanted to speak to her. Kids her age are like that. You have to take everything one step at a time.

"Can I talk to her?" I asked hopefully.

"Okay," said Claire. I heard the phone fall to the floor as she dropped it. Then I heard her footsteps as she ran off to get Mallory. It seemed to take Claire forever to find her, but I was used to waiting for Mal to come to the phone.

Somebody picked up the receiver a few minutes later, but it wasn't Mal. It was Nicky. "Who's this?" he asked.

I told him who it was. "Hi, Jessi!" he said. "Guess what! There's going to be a pet show, and Frodo's going to be in it!"

I could tell that he was really excited about it — and unlike Becca, he didn't seem to mind that he only had a hamster to enter in the show. We talked for a couple of minutes, and then Mallory picked up the phone in the kitchen.

"Okay, Nicky!" she said. "You can hang up now." We waited for a moment, but Nicky didn't hang up. I heard him breathing on the line. He was probably hoping to listen in on our conversation.

"Come on, Nicky!" said Mal. "I'll give you a dime later on if you'll hang up right now." *Click*. Finally!

"What's up, Jess?" asked Mal.

"I need your help," I said. "I just can't seem to figure out how to trap Hilary."

"Okay, let's think," said Mallory. "You can't be too obvious about it. You've got to be like that detective on TV. You know, the one who always makes the suspect feel like they have nothing to worry about, and then — *BAM!* — he gets them."

"Well, I don't think Hilary realizes that I suspect her," I said. "I've been trying to act really cool around her, so that she won't guess." It hadn't been that hard. We'd been incredibly busy at rehearsals lately.

"Good," said Mal. "Now, let's look at her personality. There must be some weakness that we can take advantage of."

"You mean, like, that she's kind of vain?" I asked. I told Mal how Hilary is always looking in the mirror to check on her fancy French braid.

"Yeah, something like that is good. Now think," said Mal. "How can we use that against her?"

"Maybe I could tell her that I thought she'd make a better Princess Aurora than me," I said, thinking out loud. "She's so vain that she'd probably agree with me, and that would almost prove that she's trying to get rid of me so that she can have the part!" I was excited.

"Jessi," said Mal, "that wouldn't really prove anything, except that she thinks she's a better dancer than you." She was silent for a moment. "No, we've got to come up with something better than that," she said. "Keep thinking."

"What if I just try to catch her off guard with some casual comment?" I asked. "Like 'Hey, thanks for all those notes you sent me!' Then, if she looks upset, that would give her away."

"It might work," said Mallory. "But you'll need witnesses, and that could get complicated. Plus, what if she just denies everything? Then you'll have totally blown it."

I had to agree that Mal was right. But I just couldn't come up with any other ideas. We talked a while longer and then said good-bye, agreeing to talk some more the next day.

After dinner that night I helped Aunt Cecelia dry the dishes. I wasn't thinking about anything in particular. Then, out of nowhere, I had this great idea. "That's it!" I said out loud. Aunt Cecelia gave me a funny look.

"*What's* it?" she asked, shaking the soapy water off her hands.

I almost wished I could talk to her about my idea, but I knew it was better not to. I hadn't told her — or my parents — anything about the phantom. It would just make them worry.

"Nothing, Aunt Cecelia," I said. "I was thinking out loud. Is it okay if I go do my homework now?"

She nodded. "We're just about done here, Jessica. Thanks for your help." She looked at me carefully, as if she knew there was something I wasn't telling her. It's not easy to fool Aunt Cecelia. She doesn't let much get past her. "Go on, now," she said finally.

I headed up to my room, but I didn't start my homework. I had something more important to think about: my Plan, with a capital P. I just knew it would work. It had to.

Here's what I had figured out: Hilary's weak spot. She was always looking for Mme Noelle's approval. Of course, everybody in the class was doing the same thing, since we all wanted to please our teacher. But Hilary really seemed to have a need for Mme Noelle to think she was perfect. Maybe it was because of her mother. Mrs. Morgan has such high expectations of Hilary.

Anyway, I thought I could somehow use that personality trait to trap Hilary. I just had to make her believe that Mme Noelle wanted her to do something — and then she'd do it without thinking.

I was really concentrating. What could Mme Noelle need from Hilary? Something that she'd have to write, of course, so that I'd know for sure that that special pen really did belong to her. And it would have to be something she'd need in a hurry, so that Hilary wouldn't have time to think about it.

A program for the performance? No, the programs were probably being printed professionally, and Hilary would know that. Invitations to our dress rehearsal? Too complicated. I had to keep it simple. What about some kind of sign?

A sign. That was it! Now my mind was racing. I pictured the scene:

Hilary writes something down. Then she realizes that she's been caught. She breaks down and confesses everything, apologizes all over the place, and tries to make me promise not to tell. But I won't. Instead, I march her in to see Mme Noelle, who tells her she's going to have to drop out of dance school. The End!

I knew that the last part of my imagined scene probably wouldn't come true. Most likely, Madame would just give Hilary a warning. But I knew that my plan would work. There was no way it could fail. I practiced over and over again how I was going to get Hilary to write something for me, until I felt that it was perfect. I couldn't wait for my next rehearsal.

Once I'd gotten my plan set, I turned to my homework. I couldn't afford to get behind in my classes, no matter how busy I was with rehearsals. But I'd only had my social studies book open for a few minutes when I heard a knock on my door.

"Come in!" I said.

The door opened slowly, and Becca peeked around it. "Can I talk to you for a minute?" she asked.

"Sure, Becca," I said. "What's the matter?" She looked upset about something. I realized suddenly that I hadn't been paying much attention to her lately. I'd been too caught up in solving the mystery of the phantom. I closed my book and told her to sit down.

"It's the pet show," she said, looking at her shoes. "I don't want to go to it."

"Becca, why not?" I asked. "It's going to be so much fun!"

"No it's not," she said. "Not if I can't win a prize."

I frowned. "But who says you won't win one?" I asked. "Misty's a great pet."

She shook her head. "I know. But she's only a hamster! How can she win any prizes? Everybody else has much better pets."

"Like who?" I asked.

"Like Charlotte," she said. "Charlotte is going to enter Carrot in the show, and Carrot can do all kinds of tricks. Did you ever see him say his prayers?"

Charlotte Johannsen is Becca's best friend. She's also one of the kids we sit for regularly. And her dog, Carrot, is pretty cute. When you tell him to say his prayers, he puts his paws in your lap and lays his head down on top of them.

"And David Michael is going to enter Shannon," continued Becca. "I'm sure Shannon will win a prize."

"Becca," I said gently, "there are going to be all kinds of pets in the show. And they all have an equal chance of winning a prize."

She didn't look convinced.

"Misty's brother is going to be in the show," I said. "And Nicky and Margo and Claire and Vanessa aren't worried about whether Frodo will win a prize. They just think the show will be fun."

I wasn't really sure about that, but it didn't hurt to say it. "And guess what Linny Papadakis is entering — a turtle!" I said. "Don't you think that's kind of funny?"

Becca shook her head, refusing to smile. I talked to her for awhile, but I couldn't convince her that winning a prize didn't matter. Finally, I just gave her a big hug and told her it was bedtime. Poor Becca. She had her heart set on winning a prize, and Misty wasn't a very impressive pet.

Then, as I was tucking her in, I had an idea. Could it work? I went back to my room and thought it over. Then I went downstairs to the phone in the kitchen. I dialed a number.

"Hello?"

"Kristy!" I said. "This is Jessi. I just got the *best* idea!"

CHAPTER 13

I told Mallory about my plan for catching Hilary while we ate lunch at school the next day. "Do you think it'll work?" I asked her.

"I don't know . . ." she said. "It sounds like your timing is going to have to be perfect if you want to catch her alone in the dressing room."

"You're right," I replied. "And I don't want to end up being late for rehearsal, either."

"Maybe you should do it *after* rehearsal," Mal said. "Does Hilary usually take a long time to get changed?"

I told Mal that she did.

"Great! Don't you think that would work better?"

I nodded. It was good to go over my plan with someone else. Mallory and I talked about it for the whole lunch period, polishing every detail until it seemed just right.

"When's your next rehearsal?" she asked, when the lunch bell rang.

I groaned. "Not until Thursday!" I couldn't believe I had to wait that long. It was only Tuesday.

"Don't worry," said Mal. "You've got a great plan, and I'm positive it's going to work."

If only I could be so sure. It was hard not to worry. This was going to be my only chance to trap Hilary. I spent the next days thinking about the plan, going over it in my head, practicing what I was going to say, and imagining how Hilary would react.

I'm sure that my parents thought something was wrong with me, but they must have chalked it up to my being nervous about the performance, which was coming up soon. At dinner I would stare into space, forgetting to eat, while I pictured Hilary's shocked face. At breakfast, I would forget what I was doing and pour the milk into my cereal bowl until it overflowed.

Aunt Cecelia seemed suspicious, too — but she didn't say anything. She just gave me sharp looks as we washed the dishes together. I tried not to show how preoccupied I was, but it was hard.

Becca got the worst of it, I'm sure. She was still upset about the pet show, which was going to be held that weekend. But I was just too distracted to give her any more consolation and advice than I already had. I was happy to hear that she had decided to go to the pet show after all, and that she was going to enter Misty. She was trying to figure out how to make her more —"special." Once, I had to stop her from trying to squeeze Misty into one of her Barbie doll's evening dresses.

Squirt was probably the only member of my family who didn't notice that there was something on my mind. Or maybe he did, and he didn't care. As long as I was around to give him "hawssy rides" (horsey rides), he didn't mind my distracted attitude.

On Tuesday night, I had a dream about trapping Hilary. In my dream, she got to her knees on the dressing room floor and begged me to forgive her.

On Wednesday afternoon we had a club meeting. I had hoped to be able to talk over my plan with everybody, but I didn't have a chance. There were too many last-minute preparations to take care of for the pet show.

On Wednesday night, I had another dream. This time, Hilary turned into a fanged monster and leaped at me when I accused her of being the phantom. I woke up with a start. What a nightmare! But I knew that, whatever else happened, there wasn't much chance that Hilary was going to turn into a monster right in front of me.

My classes dragged on Thursday, but finally school was over and it was time for rehearsal. I walked into the dressing room, and saw right away that Hilary wasn't there. I panicked. How was I going to wait a few *more* days to try out my plan? I'd never make it.

But Hilary dashed in right after I'd finished getting dressed. She was out of breath from running up the stairs. "Am I late?" she asked.

"No, but you'd better hurry," I said. "Mme Noelle just gave us the signal that she's ready to start." I almost wished that I had stuck to my original idea. At least the whole thing would be over *before* rehearsal. But it was too late now. In a moment, Mme Noelle would be taking the roll.

I grabbed my toe shoes and ran to the stage, with Hilary on my heels. Mme Noelle barely looked up as we took our places.

"We have only four rehearsals left before zee performance, mademoiselles," she said. "I osk for your complete concentration." She looked me right in the eye as she said that. I gulped. And I nodded.

But unfortunately, my concentration was terrible that day. While we were doing our warm-up exercises at the *barre*, I lost count and kicked in the wrong direction, almost knocking over Lisa.

"Sorry!" I whispered.

She smiled at me. "That's okay," she whispered back. "I'd be nervous, too, if I were playing Princess Aurora."

Little did she know that my role was the least of my worries. I shook myself and tried to forget about Hilary. If Mme Noelle noticed how distracted I was, she would be furious.

I got through the rest of the rehearsal with no major accidents. As we finished up our work for the day, I began to feel more and more nervous. What if Hilary didn't fall for my trick? What if she hadn't brought her special red pen that day? What if . . .

"You are dismissed!" said Mme Noelle, clapping her hands. "Jessica Romsey, please stay for a moment."

Oh, no! She was going to tell me how terribly I'd danced that day. Maybe she was going to take the role away from me. After everyone else had gone, I crossed to where she stood, next to the record player.

"Yes, Madame?" I asked.

"Mademoiselle Romsey, please tell me," she said. "Is everything all right? I am worrying about you." She was looking deeply into my eyes.

For a moment, just for a moment, I considered telling her everything. I'm not sure what stopped me. I guess I wanted to be able to prove what I suspected before I brought her into it. "I — I'm fine," I said. "I know my dancing has not been perfect. I'm sorry."

She smiled at me. "Even Anna Pavlova was not always perfect," she said.

Anna Pavlova is probably the most famous ballerina of all time. Every dancer wants to be "another Pavlova," including me. I smiled back at Mme Noelle. Then, suddenly, I realized that I'd better get going if I wanted to catch Hilary in the dressing room.

"May I go now?" I asked Mme Noelle.

She nodded. "But Jessica, if something is bothering you, please speak to me of it."

"Thank you!" I said. She can be so nice sometimes, even though she is a tough teacher. I guess she just expects a lot of her students. I turned and ran off the stage.

When I reached the hallway, I paused to catch my breath. This was it! I was about to unmask the phantom. Could I do it? "Go for it, Jessi!" I said to myself. Taking a deep breath, I pushed open the door of the dressing room. I looked around. It was empty. I'd blown it.

Then I heard a cough. I spun around and saw Hilary by the mirror.

"Hilary!" I said. "I'm glad you're here!"

She turned and looked at me curiously. "Why?" she asked.

I tried to sound like I was out of breath from running, which wasn't hard. My heart was pounding like crazy, just from nervousness. "It's — it's Mme Noelle," I said.

"What?" asked Hilary. "Is something wrong? Is she hurt?"

This was not going in the right direction. "No, no," I said. "Nothing like that. It's just that she needs a sign." I paused. There was something I was forgetting. "And she wants you to make it," I added, breathlessly. This wasn't going as smoothly as I'd imagined.

Hilary gave me another funny look. Then she went over to her bag and started to rummage through it. "A sign, huh?" she asked. "Okay, no problem. What should it say?"

I could have kicked myself. I'd forgotten an important part of my script! "The janitor spilled some cleaning stuff on the stairs," I said. "Mme Noelle is afraid someone will slip on it and hurt themselves before he has a chance to clean it up."

Hilary waited silently.

"So," I finished, "I guess it should just say something like 'Danger! Slippery Steps!' "

"That sounds simple enough," said Hilary.

"I'll make Mme Noelle the best sign she ever saw."

I sighed with relief. Then I saw the pen she had pulled out of her bag. It wasn't red! It was just a regular blue ballpoint. "Don't forget," I said. "It has to be highly visible, so everyone can see it."

Hilary glanced at the pen in her hand and shrugged. Then she threw it back into her bag and rummaged around some more. I almost sighed out loud. She certainly wasn't making this easy for me!

Finally, she pulled out a red pen and started to write. From where I stood, I couldn't see what the writing looked like, so I just had to wait patiently. But my heart was racing.

"How does this look?" she asked, holding the sign up for me to see. I walked over and took it from her. One glance told me that the pen she was using was the same one she'd used to write those nasty notes.

"GOTCHA!" I cried.

"What?" she asked, turning white.

"This pen!" I said. "And this writing. *You* sent me all those notes! And now I've caught you."

"What notes?" asked Hilary, narrowing her eyes. "I never sent you any notes. Just try convincing Mme Noelle that I did. It'll be your word against mine, and she'll never believe you. You can't prove anything."

"Oh, yes I can," I said. "For one thing, I've kept every note you sent me. Anyone could see that the writing is the same as the writing on that sign."

"So what?" she asked. "Why would I write you notes?"

"Because you wanted me to get so scared that I'd drop the role of Princess Aurora," I said. "You thought you'd have a chance at it if you could audition again."

"I wasn't the only one who wanted you to drop out," said Hilary.

"You're right," I said. "Katie Beth and Carrie would have liked to get that role, too. But Carrie was absent when I got a note one day, and Katie Beth saved me when you pushed that scenery onto me."

"Scenery!" said Hilary. "I didn't do that! That thing fell by accident, I swear. I didn't want you to get hurt *that* badly." Then she put her hand over her mouth. I could tell that she had realized she'd practically confessed to all her other "crimes."

"Oh, please!" she begged. "Please don't tell Mme Noelle! I couldn't stand it if I got kicked out of dance school. And my mother would be furious."

"That's why you did it in the first place,

isn't it?" I asked. "Because of your mother."

Hilary nodded. "It's so important to her for me to be a good dancer. I work really hard to live up to her expectations, but sometimes I just can't. You're a better dancer than me — that's why you got that role. But she doesn't understand."

I looked closely at Hilary. I could tell that she was about to start crying.

"I promise I won't do anything else to you, Jessi!" she said. "No more notes, no more 'accidents.' I'll leave you alone. I'll pay you back for those leotards I ruined. Just please, don't tell Madame!"

I didn't know what to do. I felt sorry for Hilary because of her mother, but I was still mad at her. I thought about it for a minute while she waited, tears in her eyes.

I was still worried that she'd try some nasty trick on me during rehearsals, or even during a performance. But since I had proof of her "crimes," she probably wouldn't. She knew she'd just be in even deeper trouble. And I realized that she had probably already suffered enough by having to deal with her awful mother.

"Okay," I said. "But don't forget that I have proof of what you did." I paused. "You'd better not try anything else, or you know what I'll do!" I tried to sound as threatening as I could, even though I didn't really know exactly what I would do to her.

Hilary was incredibly grateful. She even surrendered her calligraphy pen. "You can have this," she said. "I won't be needing it any more." Then she ran out to meet her mother.

I sat down on the dressing room bench, exhausted but happy. I'd caught the phantom! I just hoped I had done the right thing by letting her off. What if she decided to pull some last-minute trick on opening night? She might do it, just for the pleasure of seeing me look like a fool in front of the huge audience that would fill the civic center. I tried to put the thought out of my head as I went out to meet my father. I should have been feeling happy, not worried. After all, the mystery had finally been solved!

CHAPTER 14

Saturday

Well, at least we had a nice day for the pet show. Imagine if it had been raining, on top of everything else! I don't know about the rest of you guys, but I really did have a great time today – disasters and all. Still, I don't think we should make this pet show an annual event. We should remember how competitive kids can get sometimes. Jessi, your idea saved the day. Everybody went home happy.

Stacey was sitting for Charlotte Johannsen on the day of the pet show, so they arrived at Dawn and Mary Anne's early on that sunny afternoon, to help set up. Charlotte had brought Carrot with her. The little schnauzer was all spruced up. You could tell right away that he'd had a bath. And he was wearing a brand-new red collar. The leash that Charlotte was walking him on was also brand-new, and she looked pretty proud as she entered the yard.

The rest of us, except Kristy, who hadn't gotten there yet, were setting up tables for snacks and for the judges to sit at. Charlotte wanted to help, so Stacey tied Carrot to a tree.

"You be a good dog," said Charlotte. Carrot barked a few times and then curled up and went to sleep while we worked.

We set up a "ring" — a judging area in front of the judges' table — by making a circle of rocks we'd found in the driveway. Stacey surveyed it when it was done.

"It's not exactly round," she said, "but it'll have to do." Stacey was going to be one of the judges. We had decided that not every member of the club should be a judge — only those who could never be accused of being partial to one pet or another.

I couldn't be a judge because of Misty.

Kristy couldn't be a judge because Karen, Andrew, and David Michael were all going to enter pets.

Mallory couldn't be a judge because of Frodo — and because of the mystery pet that Mallory now thought the triplets were entering.

And we had decided that Mary Anne shouldn't be a judge because she loves her kitten, Tigger, so much that she might be biased toward any cats that were entered.

So that left Stacey, Claud, and Dawn as the Official Pet Show Judges.

Just as we finished setting up the snack tables, we heard a car horn honking out front. It sounded like Charlie's horn — and it was. In a second, we saw what looked like a parade coming around to the backyard. First came Charlie (with Emily Michelle riding on his shoulders) and Sam. They were going to be spectators. Behind them was Kristy, who was trying to help David Michael control Shannon. Shannon's not used to walking on a leash, and she tends to lunge all over the place.

Then there was Karen, who was proudly carrying the small cage that held Emily Junior, her rat. And next to her walked Andrew, pulling a frightened-looking Midgie (I guess he doesn't like crowds) behind him.

Stacey looked closely at Emily Junior as

Karen set the cage on one of the tables. "What's on her head?" she asked, puzzled.

"Mickey Mouse ears!" said Karen proudly. "They're her costume!"

Sure enough, Karen had cut out a tiny pair of black ears and stuck them on Emily Junior's head. Stacey stifled a laugh. "Very nice, Karen," she said. "And Andrew, this must be Midgie," she said, turning to look at him. "What a nice little dog."

Andrew looked proud. "He is nice," he said. "Even if he can't do any tricks. He's the nicest dog in the world!"

Kristy got Shannon and David Michael settled and came over to talk to the rest of us. "Are you guys ready for this?" she asked, laughing. "You should have seen us on the way over here. The car was like a three-ring circus! First Emily Junior escaped from her cage. Then, just when we'd caught her and put her back, Shannon started trying to jump out of the car at every stoplight. What a mess!"

Just then, another car pulled into the driveway. This time it was Mrs. Papadakis, who had brought Hannie and Linny with their pets, and also Scott and Timmy Hsu, who looked a little downcast.

Hannie was holding Pat the cat in her arms, and Linny was carrying Myrtle the turtle — whose shell had apparently been repainted just that morning. It looked terrific.

Kristy told Timmy and Scott that they could sit with Sam and Charlie, as spectators. "I'm glad you're here," she said. "We need an audience." They smiled at her, but they still didn't seem very happy. They looked longingly at the other pets that were being paraded around. Stacey told me later that she felt kind of sorry for them — and that she could understand since she'd never been allowed to have pets, either.

The next kids to arrive were the Delaneys, and boy, did they have a surprise for the rest of us. When Mr. Delaney pulled his car into the driveway, Amanda got out first. She was carrying a perfectly groomed Priscilla, and she was looking very possessive. Obviously, she had decided not to let Max share her pet.

Then Max climbed out of the car, and Stacey got the shock of a lifetime. In his arms was a very calm and happy-looking cat. A big, fat cat. It was Boo-Boo! And he didn't look mean at all. He looked like he'd be happy to let Max carry him around all day.

Stacey looked at Kristy and raised her eyebrows. "I know," said Kristy. "Isn't it crazy? It just seems that Boo-Boo took a liking to Max. You should hear him purring when Max pets him." Then she stopped and sniffed the air. "What *is* that smell?" she asked.

Stacey smelled it, too. "It's like that perfume my mother sometimes wears — Paris Romance, I think it's called." She looked around. "But who would have that on in the middle of the day? My mom only wears it for special occasions."

"It's Priscilla," said Amanda proudly. "Doesn't she smell lovely?" The cat must have been drenched in perfume. You couldn't get too close to her without feeling like you were going to keel over, just from the waves of fragrance that rose from her white fur.

"Lovely," said Stacey, wrinkling her nose.

By then, Dawn and Mary Anne's backyard was really filling up. A lot of barking and meowing was going on as the pets got to know each other. Stacey looked around for Charlotte and saw her standing near the tree where Carrot had been tied up. Carrot was nowhere in sight, and Charlotte looked like she was about to cry.

Stacey ran over to her. "Don't worry, Char," she said. "We'll find him." They began to walk around the yard, calling for Carrot. He wasn't near the judging circle, or by the snack table. He wasn't playing with Shannon and Midgie. "Carrot!" called Charlotte, in a teary voice.

"There he is!" said Stacey suddenly. She saw Carrot standing next to Matt and Haley Braddock, whom she hadn't seen arriving.

Matt was holding his leash. Charlotte and Stacey ran to him, and when they got closer they saw the sign that Haley was holding.

OFFICIAL HANDLERS, it said. WE'LL WATCH YOUR PET WHEN YOU NEED SOME TIME OFF.

"That's a good idea, guys," said Stacey. "But you better get permission from the owners before you start holding their pets. You had Charlotte kind of worried!"

"I'm sorry," said Haley, after signing to Matt to tell him to hand over Carrot. "We were just trying to help. Carrot looked so lonely, tied up to that tree."

Stacey smiled. "I know, but he was fine. Anyway, I'm glad you thought of a way to be part of the show. Let's go see if anyone can use your services."

As she was walking with Charlotte and the Braddocks, Stacey saw the Pikes arrive. The triplets were struggling with a large, mysterious bundle. "What's that?" she asked.

"Nothing," said Adam and Byron together.

"We were just going to put it over there," said Jordan, pointing to a large bush by the side of the house.

Stacey shrugged. "Okay," she said. "Hey, what have you got there?" she asked, turning to Nicky. He and Margo and Claire stood huddled together over a small box. Vanessa stood off to the side, looking like she wanted nothing to do with her younger brothers and sisters.

"It's Frodo," said Nicky.

"And wait till you see what they did to him," added Vanessa. "Show Stacey," she said to Nicky.

Nicky opened the lid of the box. Stacey peered in, then jumped back. "What was that green thing?" she asked.

"That's Frodo," said Nicky proudly.

"They got into the dyes my mom uses for cake frostings," said Vanessa, rolling her eyes. "Can you believe it?"

Stacey looked again and laughed. "He looks pretty funny," she said. "But it *is* different, I have to say that!"

"It *is* different," said Becca, who had just appeared next to Nicky. She was looking enviously at Frodo's bright green fur. "I wish I'd thought of that." She held up Misty, who looked like a regular hamster — one who had had her hair combed neatly.

"Misty looks nice," said Stacey. Then trying to change the subject, she said, "Look, here come the Barretts, with Pow." Sure enough, there were Suzi and Buddy, walking Pow, who was covered with pink ribbons. He looked a little silly, but Suzi and Buddy seemed proud.

Stacey barely had a chance to say hello to

them before Kristy and Dawn ran up to her, out of breath. "Have you seen Myrtle?" Kristy asked. "He ran off, and Linny is so upset."

A search party was organized. Matt and Haley were given dogs to hold while their owners ran around the yard, looking for the turtle. Linny looked like he was about to cry as he crawled under some bushes. "Myrtle!" he called. "Where are you?"

Just then there was a shout. Timmy Hsu held up Myrtle as he yelled, "I found her! I found her!" Myrtle had been sitting among the rocks in the judging circle, her painted shell blending with the dandelions that spotted the lawn.

"Thanks, Timmy," said Linny. "Listen, you can be Myrtle's part owner, just for today, okay?"

Timmy nodded happily, but his smile faded as he glanced at Scott, who was standing to one side, looking sad. Then Hannie spoke up. "Scott, since you're my husband, I guess you can be part owner of Pat the cat."

By that time, it looked like just about everybody had arrived. Gabbie and Myriah were the last to come. They had spent their morning running after Chewy, who had, as usual, pulled his leash right out of their hands.

"I think we're ready to begin the judging,"

said Kristy loudly. Her voice was barely audible over the noise that all those kids and their pets were making.

The rest of us helped to round up the kids and get them into line for the parade past the judges. After the parade, each pet would be shown briefly in the judging circle. Then the judges would consult with each other and the prizes would be announced.

Everybody got quiet as they led their pets past the judges' table. The tension increased as each pet had its time in the ring. Some pets, like Carrot, did tricks for the judges. Others just sat there, looking — or in Priscilla's case, smelling — pretty.

We'd all forgotten about the triplets' mystery pet until Adam ran to the judges to tell them that there was a late entry. Then he ran back to the bush where the bundle had been left and reappeared, leading — a pony! Jordan and Byron were dressed up as the front and back of a horse, and Adam led them proudly past the judges' table. The pony pranced and bucked and kicked until the kids and the judges were nearly hysterical.

After the judging, Kristy led the pet owners to the snack table while the judges conferred. I saw Becca looking nervous as she ate a cookie and waited for the results. But she had nothing to be nervous about. Guess why. Because of my idea. Here's what it was: Every pet in the show would get a prize — not first prize or second prize, just a prize that said something about why that pet was special.

The idea was a total success. I saw a lot of happy faces when the judges announced the prizes, starting with "Most Unusually Colored Pet," for Frodo, and going on through "Best-Smelling" (guess which white cat won that) and "Smartest." (Carrot won that one.)

"Funniest Pet" went to the triplets, while "Largest Pet" was awarded to Shannon. "Nicest Pet" went to Midgie, and Myrtle won "Prettiest Shell." Karen was thrilled when Emily Junior won "Best Costume," and Scott and Hannie looked proud when Pat the cat won "Cutest." Pow won "Shortest Legs."

Gabby and Myriah laughed when Chewy was named "Strongest Pet," and even Matt and Haley got a prize for being "Best Pet Handlers." Boo-Boo won for "Best Personality." (*That* was a surprise!) And what did Becca win? Well, I predict that Misty's ribbon will be hanging in Becca's room for a long, long time. Here's what it says: "Best All-Around Pet."

CHAPTER 15

Opening Night. I think that those two words may be the most exciting in the English language. I get a chill just hearing them. And now it was finally here. Opening Night.

We'd had a pretty good dress rehearsal earlier in the week. A few small problems were ironed out that night. For example, my tutu. I think someone mixed up my measurements with the ones belonging to Jumbo the circus elephant. But that's what dress rehearsal is for. And Aunt Cecelia had no trouble taking it in for me. By opening night, my tutu fit perfectly.

"Try it on for me one more time!" begged Becca. She loves to see me all dressed up like a "real" ballerina.

"There's no time," I said. "You'll see me in it when I come onstage. But remember, you have to be quiet while I'm dancing." Once, when Becca was younger and I was dancing in *The Nutcracker*, she'd yelled, "Hi, Jessi!" when I made my entrance. Everybody in the audience laughed, and I almost died of embarrassment.

"I won't," she promised. "Don't forget that you promised to give me your toe shoes after the show."

I was going to autograph them and give them to her for a souvenir. That's what the really famous ballerinas do for their fans. Toe shoes usually can't be worn for more than one or two performances — they just don't last under that kind of use.

"Ready, Jessi?" my mom called up the stairs. "I think your friends are here."

I looked out the window and saw Charlie's car parked in the street. He was going to drive my friends to the performance. But why were they here? I was going to be driving with my parents.

I ran downstairs and out the door. My friends had gotten really dressed up for the occasion. "Wow, you guys look great!" I said.

"So do you," said Kristy. I was wearing my black velvet dress. I wanted to have something nice to change into after the performance.

Claudia looked extremely cool and exotic, as usual. Her hair was braided with silver ribbons, and she wore a shimmery dark blue minidress. On her feet were silver sandals, with laces up the calves — kind of like toe shoes.

Stacey had on a tuxedo! That's right, a tuxedo, just like one a boy would wear. But it was made to fit her perfectly, and she looked great. She must have gotten it in New York.

Kristy had put on a dress, for once, and it was strange to see her in something other than a turtleneck and jeans. She looked really pretty. And Mallory, standing next to her in her best skirt and blouse, looked great, too. Dawn and Mary Anne must have traded clothes — they do that a lot — because I recognized Mary Anne's new Laura Ashley dress on Dawn, and Dawn's pink jumpsuit on Mary Anne.

"We just came by to wish you luck," said Mallory. "I know you're going to do a great job. We can't wait to see you dance!"

"And don't worry about you-know-who," said Dawn. "I'm sure she won't pull anything."

I nodded. But I wasn't so sure. I was still worried about Hilary. It wouldn't take much to ruin my performance and make me look like a jerk in front of everybody. She'd only have to give me a shove, or spill something on the stage before I went on. I just didn't trust her.

"Thanks for coming by, you guys," I said. "I'll see you after the show, okay? You're all invited backstage."

"Great!" said Stacey. "Break a — " Then she stopped. "I can't say it," she said.

I was just as glad. I was worried that if somebody said "break a leg" I really might, especially if Hilary decided to pull one of her tricks. I waved at my friends as they got back into the car. "Have fun!" I yelled, as they drove off. By then, Becca had come out of the house. She grabbed my hand and pulled me over to the car.

"I have a surprise for you," she said. "But I'm not going to tell yet. I promised." I wondered what she was talking about. She looked very excited. She also looked very cute, dressed in her ruffly pink party dress.

I got into the car to wait for Mama and Daddy and Aunt Cecelia, but then I jumped back out. I'd forgotten to say good-bye to Squirt! Logan was going to sit for him so that the rest of my family could come to the ballet.

Mama was just telling Logan about Squirt's bedtime when I burst through the door. Squirt was sitting in his high chair, and I picked him up carefully after making sure that he didn't have too much food on his face (he was eating creamed spinach). " 'Bye, Squirt," I said, kissing him. "Wish me luck!"

157

"Uck," said Squirt. I laughed.

"Do you think he's wishing me luck, or just telling us what he thinks of creamed spinach?" I asked Mama.

"I don't know," she said, laughing. "But we'd better get going. All set, Logan?"

He nodded.

And then it was time to leave. We piled into the car and drove to the civic center. In the parking lot, I said good-bye to my family. Then I went through the backstage entrance.

Backstage before a performance is an exciting place. People are running around and yelling things like, "Where's the blue filter for the spotlight?" and, "Has anyone seen my tiara?" Some of my classmates had already changed into their costumes and were warming up in the wings. The orchestra was making tootling noises in the pit in front of the stage.

I took a minute to peek around the curtain. The audience looked huge! At first I couldn't find my family. Where were they? Then I spotted them, sitting in the middle of the third row. And my friends were seated right behind them. I waved to Mallory, but I knew she couldn't see me. Then I ran to the dressing room.

I changed into my costume carefully, making sure not to rip out any of Aunt Cecelia's careful stitches. I was wearing a brand-new pair of pink tights, to match my pink tutu. After I'd braided my hair, I pinned on my headpiece — a crown of roses. Later I'd replace it with a (fake) diamond tiara, but for the Rose Adagio I wore flowers in my hair.

I decided to do my makeup before getting into my toe shoes, so I sat down at the big mirror that ran across the wall of the dressing room. As I was putting on some blusher (which I never get to wear in real life), I looked behind myself in the mirror and saw Hilary looking right at me. She smiled shyly when she caught my eye.

"Good luck," she said. "You look beautiful."

"Thanks," I said cautiously. "So do you." Did she really mean it? Or was she just trying to throw me off?

I finished my makeup and then took one last look in the mirror. Suddenly I didn't look like Jessi Ramsey, sixth-grade baby-sitter anymore. I looked like a ballerina.

The pink tutu was fluffed out perfectly around my waist. The crown of roses sat elegantly on my head. And my face looked — different. Older, more sophisticated. I hardly recognized myself.

"Five minutes!" yelled somebody from outside the dressing room door. Oh, my lord! I hadn't even warmed up yet! For a minute I felt totally panicked. Then I remembered. I wasn't even in the first act! I had plenty of time.

I ran to the wings, carrying my toe shoes. All of the dancers who were in the first act were already arranged on the stage. The curtain went up, and the orchestra began to play. I heard applause from the audience. Then the ballet began.

I watched the first act as I put on my toe shoes and did my warming-up exercises. I was beginning to get caught up in the story — the story I'd almost forgotten during those weeks of rehearsal. I'd gotten totally involved in practicing my steps over and over again, and the wonderful fairy tale of the Sleeping Beauty had become less important. But now it was coming to life.

On the stage, the king and queen sat on thrones while each fairy danced a special dance as she presented a gift to the baby princess. Then, just as the Lilac Fairy was about to present her gift, the bad fairy, Carabosse, appeared in a coach drawn by four giant rats. (The rats were dancers from the beginner's classes.) She shrieked and cackled as she danced, screaming at the king and queen because they had not invited her to the baby's christening.

The king and queen begged her forgiveness, but she would not listen. Instead, she put a curse on the baby princess — that she would one day prick her finger on a spindle and die.

All the dancers fell back when Carabosse cursed the baby — except for the Lilac Fairy. Lisa looked beautiful in her costume as she stepped forward with her wand held high, driving Carabosse back and trying to remove the curse. The Lilac Fairy couldn't take the curse off, but she did manage to change it, so that instead of dying, the princess would only sleep — for a hundred years, until a handsome prince woke her up.

I was completely caught up in the story by the time the first act ended and the "fairies" came rushing off the stage. Then I heard the music that was my cue. I took a deep breath and walked onto the stage. I hoped I looked like a real princess — like Princess Aurora, on her sixteenth birthday.

The Rose Adagio began, and almost immediately, I was swept into the dance so completely that my nervousness fell away. I didn't worry about Hilary. I didn't worry about whether Becca was going to call my name. And I didn't worry about whether my friends were having a good time. I just danced.

At the end of the second act, Carabosse came back onstage. She tempted me with her spindle, and when I took it I pricked my finger and collapsed into my hundred-year sleep. The rest of the dancers put me into a bed, and the "magic forest" grew up around me as I slept.

Next, I danced for the prince who had come looking for me one hundred years later. Of course, I was only supposed to be a vision — a dream. He kept trying to dance with me, but I kept escaping from his embrace.

Then I had a rest, as the prince journeyed to find me, led by the Lilac Fairy. And then he found me and kissed me. I didn't giggle at all. (My friends probably did.) I woke up and danced with all the fairy tale creatures, including Carrie as the Bluebird of Happiness. That part was especially fun.

Then, at the end, I danced with the prince, who was now my husband. The dancer who played him was from another class. I think he's an eighth-grader. He's a good dancer, and very strong. That's important in this dance, because he keeps having to lift me up in the air.

The music in that part is so pretty that I could have danced forever. But finally, the music ended and the performance was over. Carrie hugged me as soon as the curtain came down.

"You were *great!*" she said.

"So were you," I answered. "Do you think they liked us?" I listened to the applause. It had started immediately, and it didn't stop as we took our first curtain call.

"I guess they did!" she said to me, as the curtain went down again.

When we took our second curtain call, she pushed me out in front of the line of dancers. I'd almost forgotten that I was supposed to curtsy by myself. When I did, the applause swelled, and I heard Kristy's whistle. My dad was yelling "Bravo!" I smiled, and looked to my right. There, in the wings, was Mme Noelle. She smiled back at me. She looked proud.

Then I looked back at the audience. People were starting to stand up — but they weren't leaving. They were still clapping. A standing ovation! I'd never gotten one before. I felt the tears come to my eyes. And then I saw Becca, her arms full of pink roses, climbing the stairs to the stage.

She walked across the stage and handed them to me, smiling. "Surprise!" she whispered. I took the roses and gave her a huge hug. She'd kept that secret very well. When I let her go, I looked up to see Mallory standing there with another bouquet of roses — white ones. (I guess she knew how I felt about red roses!) "These are from everybody in the club," she said, handing them to me. "You were wonderful!"

I was speechless. I stood with my arms full of roses, smiling out at the audience, until the curtain fell again. I will never forget that moment!

Then the show was really over. It was time to get out of my costume, wash the makeup off my face, and go back to being Jessi.

I headed for the dressing room and ran into Hilary in the hall. "Jessi, you were fantastic!" she said.

"So were you. So was everybody," I answered. "Wasn't it fun?" I'd almost forgotten that I'd ever been worried about Hilary and her dirty tricks.

"I want to apologize again," she said. "I'm really sorry for what I did. And you know what? After this, I'm quitting dance."

I was shocked. "You're kidding!" I said.

"Nope," she answered. "I never really loved it. Not like you do. I mainly did it for my mother. And I just wasn't that good at it."

"You are too good," I said. I didn't like to hear her put herself down.

"Not good enough for my mother," Hilary replied. "And I realized that things had gotten out of hand that day when you confronted me in the dressing room. I must have been crazy to do the things I did to you."

"How does your mother feel about your quitting?" I asked.

She frowned. "I haven't told her yet. But it's my life, and I have to do what I want."

I gave her a hug. "Good luck," I said. "I'll miss you in class." And as soon as I said it, I knew it was true. I would miss her. Hilary's okay. And maybe once she quits dance her mother will go easier on her.

When I walked into the dressing room, I saw my friends from the BSC waiting for me. They rushed over to hug me and tell me how wonderful the ballet had been.

"Anybody up for ice cream?" I asked, after I'd thanked them for the flowers. My dad had said that I could invite my friends out for a celebration after the performance.

"Sounds great!" said Mallory, and everyone else agreed. After I'd changed, we walked out of the theater together to meet my family. Becca threw herself at me, and I gave her the toe shoes I'd worn in the show.

"Did you autograph them?" she asked.

"Sure did," I said, smiling at Mama and Daddy and Aunt Cecelia, who were standing nearby, waiting their turn to hug me. "See? Right there."

I pointed to my left toe shoe, where I'd written (in red ink, with the calligraphy pen that no longer cursed me), "For Becca, with love from Princess Aurora."

About the Author

ANN M. MARTIN did *a lot* of baby-sitting when she was growing up in Princeton, New Jersey. Now her favorite baby-sitting charge is her cat, Mouse, who lives with her in her Manhattan apartment.

Ann Martin's Apple Paperbacks include *Yours Turly, Shirley; Ten Kids, No Pets; With You and Without You; Bummer Summer;* and all the other books in the Baby-sitters Club series.

She is a former editor of books for children, and was graduated from Smith College. She likes ice cream, the beach, and *I Love Lucy;* and she hates to cook.

Look for # 43

STACEY'S EMERGENCY

That evening Dad ordered two kinds of salad and some sandwiches from a nearby deli. We ate dinner in the kitchen, which was much more relaxing than eating out, even at the Sign of the Dove. I changed into jeans, and Dad and I just sat around and talked and ate.

I considered calling Laine, but by nine o'clock I was so relaxed that I yawned and said, "I think I'll go to bed now."

"Now?" Dad looked surprised.

"Yeah, I'm really zonked." Thirsty, too, but I didn't say so.

It was hard to hide this from Dad, though. His apartment is not all that big. There's only one bathroom, and it's closer to his bedroom than to mine. So he heard me when I kept getting up all night for drinks of water.

Once during the night, Dad was waiting for me when I came out of the bathroom. "Are you okay?" he asked. "I knew we shouldn't have ordered from the deli."

"Oh, my stomach's fine," I answered. "It's just that I'm still so thirsty. I keep drinking water and then I have to go to the bathroom all the time."

Dad frowned. "We should check your blood sugar level."

"Now?" It was three-thirty. "No way. I'm falling asleep. Tomorrow." I made my getaway as quickly as I could.

But by the next morning, when I was still drinking like crazy, Dad didn't even suggest checking my blood sugar again. He just said, "I think it's time to call the doctor, don't you?"

I nodded. Something was very wrong. I couldn't deny it any longer.

Dad ran for the phone. When he couldn't reach my doctor immediately, he put me in a cab and we rode to the nearest hospital.

Win a Totally Fabulous

VIDEO!

Wow! Imagine your favorite Baby-sitters on TV! You can win a live-action **Baby-sitters Club Video** starring Kristy, Stacey, Mary Anne, and the rest of the gang in all-new **Baby-sitters Club** adventures! Just fill in the coupon below and return it by May 31, 1991!

25 Winners!

- -

The Baby-sitters Club Video Giveaway

Name_____

Address_____

City _____ State_____ Zip_____

Where did you buy this *Baby-sitters Club* book?

❑ Bookstore ❑ Drugstore ❑ Supermarket ❑ Library

❑ Book Club ❑ Book Fair ❑ Other_____ (specify)

BSC990

THE BABY-SITTERS CLUB®

by Ann M. Martin

The Baby-sitters' business is booming! And that gets Stacey, Kristy, Claudia, and the rest of The Baby-sitters Club members in all kinds of adventures…at school, with boys, and, of course, baby-sitting!

Something new and exciting happens in every Baby-sitters Club book. Collect and read them all!

More titles… ▶

☐	MG42501-3	#28	Welcome Back, Stacey!	$2.95
☐	MG42500-5	#29	Mallory and the Mystery Diary	$2.95
☐	MG42498-X	#30	Mary Anne and the Great Romance	$2.95
☐	MG42497-1	#31	Dawn's Wicked Stepsister	$2.95
☐	MG42496-3	#32	Kristy and the Secret of Susan	$2.95
☐	MG42495-5	#33	Claudia and the Great Search	$2.95
☐	MG42494-7	#34	Mary Anne and Too Many Boys	$2.95
☐	MG42508-0	#35	Stacey and the Mystery of Stoneybrook	$2.95
☐	MG43565-5	#36	Jessi's Baby-sitter	$2.95
☐	MG43566-3	#37	Dawn and the Older Boy	$2.95
☐	MG43567-1	#38	Kristy's Mystery Admirer	$2.95
☐	MG43568-X	#39	Poor Mallory!	$2.95
☐	MG43569-8	#40	Claudia and the Middle School Mystery	$2.95
☐	MG43570-1	#41	Mary Anne Versus Logan	$2.95
☐	MG44240-6		Baby-sitters on Board! Super Special #1	$3.50
☐	MG44239-2		Baby-sitters' Summer Vacation Super Special #2	$3.50
☐	MG43973-1		Baby-sitters' Winter Vacation Super Special #3	$3.50
☐	MG42493-9		Baby-sitters' Island Adventure Super Special #4	$3.50
☐	MG43575-2		California Girls! Super Special #5	$3.50
☐	MG43745-3		The Baby-sitters Club 1990-91 Student Planner and Date Book	$7.95
☐	MG43744-5		The Baby-sitters Club 1991 Calendar	$8.95
☐	MG43803-4		The Baby-sitters Club Notebook	$1.95

Available wherever you buy books...or use this order form.

Scholastic Inc., P.O. Box 7502, 2931 E. McCarty Street, Jefferson City, MO 65102

Please send me the books I have checked above. I am enclosing $_____
(please add $2.00 to cover shipping and handling). Send check or money order — no cash or C.O.D.s please.

Name _____

Address _____

City _____ State/Zip_____

Please allow four to six weeks for delivery. Offer good in the U.S. only. Sorry, mail orders are not available to residents of Canada. Prices subject to change.

Invite a "Little Sister" to join the

Little Sister™

Birthday Club!

Do you know a Baby-sitters Little Sister fan? Pass along this page and she can join the **Baby-sitters Little Sister Birthday Club!** Then on her birthday, she'll receive a personalized card from Karen herself!

That's not all! Every month, a **BIRTHDAY KID OF THE MONTH** will be randomly chosen to **WIN** a complete set of *Baby-sitters Little Sister* books! The first book in the set will be autographed by author Ann M. Martin!

Fill in the coupon or write the information on a 3" x 5" piece of paper and mail to:
BABY-SITTERS LITTLE SISTER BIRTHDAY CLUB, Scholastic Inc.,
730 Broadway, P.O. Box 742, New York, New York 10003.
Offer expires March 31, 1992.

- -

Baby-sitters Little Sister Birthday Club

❑ **YES!** I want to join the BABY-SITTERS LITTLE SISTER BIRTHDAY CLUB!

My birthday is_____.

Name_____ Age_____

Street _____

City_____State_____ Zip_____

P.S. Please put your birthday on the *outside* of your envelope too! Thanks!

Where did you buy this book?

❑ Bookstore   ❑ Drugstore   ❑ Supermarket   ❑ Library
❑ Book Club   ❑ Book Fair   ❑ Other_____(specify)

BSC990